THE SILENT HEART

THE SILENT HEART

Chapter 1

"What is going on here?" Laura asked bemusedly as she approached the small group of women, dropped her purse on her desk, set her camera beside it, and leaned back to watch her friend Karen gesturing gracefully to the others. "And who's the gorgeous hunk?"

"That's what I want to know," Katrina said, her glossy mouth nearly frothing with curiosity. "Interpret for me, Laura. I'm still so slow at this!"

Laura grinned as she shrugged out of her coat and scarf, chafing some warmth back into hands chilled by an Illinois January wind. Katrina was like a shark in a feeding frenzy, when a handsome man was around. One nibble on him and she was ready to devour any and all men in sight. "All right," Laura said, adjusting the silver comb that held her cornsilk blond hair in place off her face. She liked to wear her long and wavy hair loose about her shoulders.

Laura faced Karen and began interpreting her sign language. "There's a real hunk in Beth's office. Tall, dark, and handsome, with blue eyes that could melt ice cubes at fifty yards." Laura laughed. Karen was prone to exaggeration.

Quickly she signed back to Karen, *He sounds like Superman.* Karen nodded with a smile and Laura grinned.

Katrina was tapping her long manicured nails on Laura's arm to get her attention. "Find out who he is, for heaven's sake!" she pleaded when Laura looked at her.

Laura spoke to Karen in sign language, simultaneously voicing out loud what she was saying with her hands. "Beth's appointment book says he's David Evers" — Karen spelled out the name letter by letter — "and he's here about us running a feature on his house in the magazine." Laura looked at Katrina and shrugged. Karen tugged her sleeve and signed. *And he's running in the state senate primary.*

"Great," Laura said sarcastically. "A politician."

Karen finished by placing her hands over her heart and fluttering her eyelashes. "My sentiments exactly," Katrina said when Laura looked at her.

Laura shook her head. "Deliver me from politicians."

"In that case," Katrina said, brightening, "get out of my way, girls, and let a master go to work." She plucked a compact from her pocket and studied her makeup. Laura caught a glimpse of her own hazel eyes in the mirror before the compact snapped shut, and noted with surprise that she looked angry. Well, she'd certainly never had a fondness for politicians. Not after Buddy.

8

"You two plan your assault on the hunk," she told them. "I've got some photos to develop." She picked up her camera and headed for the darkroom, struck again by how Karen had bloomed since Beth had hired her at *Springfield Today*. Laura was training Karen as a photographer herself; Beth had already used several of Karen's pictures in the monthly magazine. Laura closed the door and flipped the switch to turn on the red "in use" light outside. In five minutes, she'd completely forgotten the alleged hunk of their discussion, as she worked on her pictures.

In Beth Aarons's office, David Evers found his eyes straying to the attractive blonde outside, although he tried to concentrate on Beth's pitch for why *Springfield Today* should photograph his Frank Lloyd Wright house. He was a little cynical about beautiful women. After being out of the dating race for a number of years, it seemed now that most women who looked like that were grooming themselves to become a man's second wife, the wife who got all the goodies after the first one. And it left a bad taste in his mouth. Just the other day one of the other editors where he worked had introduced his new wife, a bubbly redhead, who from the looks of her jewelry had a serious appetite for sapphires. And credit cards. Jack had said something humorous about how she had insisted on getting his credit limit raised, but his wife hadn't looked as though it was a joke to her.

He started when Beth asked him a question, and he had to replay the conversation quickly in his head before he could answer. Even so, when Beth began speaking again he found his eyes wandering back to the blonde. God, she had an animated face! She was translating for another girl there who was apparently deaf, and her expression lit up alternately with laughter, mischievousness, and a flash of anger that surprised him. What could they be talking about? She was wearing a peach-colored dress that clung to her hips as she moved, and he found himself mesmerized by her. David watched as she walked to a little room nearby and closed the door. Reluctantly, he turned his attention back to Beth.

Laura was gingerly checking the prints soaking in solution when light suddenly flooded the room. She spun around in annoyance. "Close the door! I'm developing pictures!"

The door was still open, and she could see a large figure in the doorway. The figure hesitantly came inside. She could tell it was a man, but she couldn't see him all that clearly with him blocking the light. "The door," she told him testily. "You know, the big thing with hinges? Take the knob and — oh, never mind."

She breezed past him and pushed the door shut, catching a whiff of a clean, masculine scent as she did so. *Nice,* her nose registered even as her mind sent up warning signals.

He was saying something, but she couldn't see

very well and gestured for him to wait a minute. "Well, the pictures weren't important anyway," she said with a sigh. "I was experimenting with light effects." She flipped on the overhead light and stood back to study the man who had ruined her photos. *Hunk* was the first word that came to mind, and she remembered Karen's evaluation of the man in Beth's office. Was this the same man?

"I'm sorry," he said, looking genuinely contrite. "I didn't know this was a darkroom."

"Well, so much for the red light over the door," she said. "Didn't you see it?"

"Pardon me?"

Laura sighed. "Never mind. We'll add being colorblind to your attributes."

"You think I have attributes, do you?" he asked, interested.

"No," she said dryly. "I think you don't know a darkroom from a horse's patootie." She tried to keep her eyes firmly on his mouth, but they insisted on wandering away, lingering on the broad shoulders, slim waist and hips, and long legs, all beautifully packaged in a charcoal gray suit. She marshaled her eyes back to his lips again in time to see him say, "Ah, so you're an anatomy expert too."

Laura flushed before she realized he was talking about her reference to horses and not her wayward eyes, which were now taking inventory of his face. Dark brown hair that looked thick and lustrous, eyebrows the same color. He must

11

have been about thirty-five. His nose was a trifle long and just the smallest bit crooked, but it only added to his blatant handsomeness. And his eyes — they were so blue! Yet, the longer she looked into them they almost seemed gray.

"I'm not used to visiting darkrooms," he said, and she focused on his mouth again. It was a nice, firm mouth with a full lower lip . . . Never mind what his mouth looks like, Laura, she scolded herself. You've focused on enough of them in your twenty-nine years.

When she didn't say anything, he added, "I usually just holler at photographers from the safety of distance. I don't venture into their lairs. My name's David Evers," he said, holding out his hand. "I'm a newspaper editor."

"And a candidate," Laura said dryly, shaking his hand.

"Gosh, does it show?" he asked, checking behind himself as if expecting to find a sign pinned to his back. Laura had to smile at him.

"My name is Laura Kincaid," she said.

"How do you do, Laura Kincaid," he said, grinning at her. "Listen, are you busy tonight? There's a local symphony concert. They're quite good. I noticed you before and, well — I'd love some company." She tried not to be bowled over by his considerable charm.

"I don't think so, thank you," Laura said, frowning and turning back to her ruined pictures, making a show of picking them up and shaking her head over their demise.

David watched her and thought again how attractive she was and how unaware of it she seemed. Her face was suffused with emotion when she talked, and although she had slurred her words slightly, her voice was low and full of laughter. He realized, not for the first time lately, that he was badly in need of some laughter. "How about dinner then?" he asked. Laura didn't even turn around. He was striking out here and he wasn't sure why. Not that he was an experienced asker-out of women. He'd hardly said hello to a woman since Barbara died. But something about this woman had compelled him. He suddenly felt she'd like nothing more than to hustle him out of her darkroom.

"You do eat, don't you?" he asked, coming to stand beside her.

"What?" she said in distraction, looking up at him. Her hair cascaded over her right shoulder when she turned, and he noticed a small, light tan object nestled in her ear. She was wearing a hearing aid. And he — clueless as he was — had just invited her to a concert. His eye rested on the plastic form a moment longer, then slid to her eyes. A warm shade of hazel. He realized she was watching his mouth, not his eyes. And with that came the realization that she was lipreading.

He put his hands in his pockets, and rocked on his heels. "Listen," he said, "I'm sorry about the concert. I'd probably fall asleep anyway. I just wanted to impress you with how sophisticated I am. How about dinner instead? I know a great place that I really like . . . maybe you would, too."

He seemed so earnest that Laura made the mistake of letting her eyes make contact with his. And she was impressed. She didn't like politicians, she told herself. No sincerity, no warmth. But even as she told that to herself, she knew that this particular politician seemed to be genuinely sorry he'd asked a woman with almost no hearing to a concert.

"I don't think so," she said, trying to soften her refusal with a smile.

"I usually get stuck eating greasy fried stuff," he told her, pulling a sorrowful face. "All those campaign dinners, you know. And then there are those awful fast-food hamburgers — loaded with cholesterol. I guess I'll just choke another one down tonight, since I'll be eating all alone." He looked at her hopefully.

"All right," she said, laughing. "Dinner. What are you going to impress me with there, the wine list?"

He shook his head, grinning. "Wait and see. I'll pick you up here about six. Is that okay?"

"Fine," she said, lowering her head and pretending to fuss with the photos.

The door opened again, and Laura looked around. David Evers had already gone, and Katrina was wandering in, looking over her shoulder at him in rapture.

"What now?" Laura sighed.

"What did you do?" Katrina demanded.

14

"Leave a trail of perfume to this place? Before I could even bat an eyelash he was in here."

"That's because the man — like other people around here — doesn't know what a darkroom is," Laura said pointedly.

Katrina rolled her eyes. "You and your precious darkroom. Here. I shot this roll of film this morning."

Laura took it with a grumbled promise to develop it before she left that evening. Katrina's shots were almost always of men in various states of undress; and the more undressed the man, the more Katrina liked it. This roll was probably shot at the local health club.

No sooner had the door closed behind Katrina than it opened again. Laura turned around in exasperation. "Is this Grand Central Station or what!" she demanded of Beth.

"What's wrong?" Beth asked innocently.

"What's wrong is that everyone in this office has been traipsing in and out of here with no regard for the red light."

"What red light?" Beth asked.

Laura stalked to the door and poked her head out. The light was off. "My light burned out," she announced to no one in particular. It struck her then that David Evers could have lambasted her right back when she lit into him about opening her door when the light was on — but he hadn't. Either he was practicing in never alienating a potential voter, she thought — or else he was just a nice man.

15

"When you get done in here come in my office," Beth said. Her friend gave no indication she'd heard a thing. "Laura, are you all right? Is your hearing aid working?"

"Yes." Laura nodded wryly. "I need to get the thing checked, but I've been busy. I've got an appointment next month with my otologist. Come on. I'm done in here."

Laura sat down in the chair opposite Beth's desk, hiding her smile when Beth broke out a box of expensive chocolates. "You know," Laura observed mischievously, "if we were men that would be a bottle of scotch."

"Ummmph," Beth said around a piece of candy. "This is called female bonding. And don't touch the butter toffees. They're all mine."

"Yes, boss," Laura said, reaching for a dark chocolate piece. Beth was in her early fifties. She and Laura had met years before in the speech therapist's office. Laura had been there on her usual visit and Beth had brought her mother, who'd had a stroke. It was Beth who had encouraged Laura in her study of photography and had given her the job at *Springfield Today*. Beth was always about to start a diet — as soon as she finished her next meal, of course.

"David Evers was in here today," Beth began.

"He was in my darkroom, too," Laura said lightly. The memory of dark blue eyes and a kind smile came rushing back, and she bit into her chocolate when she felt her pulse pick up like a

Thoroughbred rounding the home stretch. Chocolate always did make her heart pound, she reasoned.

Beth raised her eyebrows but didn't comment right away. "We're going to feature his Frank Lloyd Wright house in the August issue, and I want you to do the pictures."

Laura took a deep breath. Dinner was one thing. But photographing a man's house meant learning to know him intimately. Laura had found she could tell more about someone from his home than from anything he might tell her. And she wasn't sure she wanted to delve into the private David Evers. "I don't know," she said slowly.

"Oh, come on," Beth cajoled. "Look, the guy's a real looker, charming as hell, and I just happened to notice that he couldn't keep his eyes off you while he was in my office."

Laura had to smile. "He also found me in the darkroom and invited me to dinner."

"Oh, saints preserve us!" Beth enthused, rolling her eyes and making Laura laugh. "The man definitely has taste, not to mention good looks, too."

"Beth!" Laura teased. "It seems a lot of guys look good to you."

"And you, my dear, have not had a date in the last ten months. And don't contradict me, because I keep track of these things. My cat has more of a social life than you do, and he's been neutered."

Laura laughed again, then sobered. "Beth," she said softly. "I feel like I've finally found myself. I don't need *this* in my life now."

"If *this* means David Evers, then no, I suppose you don't actually need him right now."

"He's a politician, Beth. That means publicity and shaking hands and smiling at people on days when you'd rather run and hide from them. I had enough of that circus to last a lifetime."

Beth sighed. She looked contrite for about ten seconds and then pleaded, "Laura, couldn't you admit you like the man just a teeny tiny bit, just enough to give your old friend Beth an active fantasy life? Then I could enjoy a love affair without the attendant miseries of actually being involved in it myself."

"Sure — leave *me* to suffer the miseries," Laura said lightly.

"You're thinking about Buddy, aren't you?" Beth said seriously. "Laura, from what I know of David Evers, he's nothing like Buddy."

Laura shrugged. "I don't know. I always thought that any man who sought the limelight, be it in politics, TV, or whatever, was looking for public affection because he didn't give or get enough love at home."

"Buddy wasn't typical of the species," Beth said, idly toying with another piece of candy. "And, from what you've said, he did his best to make you feel guilty about 'not getting enough love.' The Fielding School for the Deaf is in the past now. I don't think David Evers is on the same kind of ego trip." She tapped her nails on the desk and said, "I won't ask you to make up your mind about taking those pictures right away. See how you feel after dinner tonight." She winked at Laura and was rewarded with a smile.

"All right. I'll think about it." Laura stood up and started for the door, but she couldn't resist looking back over her shoulder. Beth was communing with her box of chocolates, alternately fingering a toffee and a buttercream. "Oh, and Beth," Laura said as seriously as she could. "You're a real trouper sticking with this new diet you're on."

Beth pretended to throw a piece of candy at Laura as she laughed, and then popped it into her mouth instead.

Karen came up the aisle as Laura headed back to her desk, grinning. Karen signed that she'd taken some pictures of some of the kids at the Hastings Institute, and could Laura please print them for her? Laura told her sure, and took the film to the darkroom.

Later, as she worked over the chemical trays, she smiled at the emerging faces. Eager and enthusiastic, sometimes quiet and reflective, often filled with intensity, these were the kids she'd come to love. The Hastings Institute. It was a long way from the Fielding School for the Deaf. Then again, it was a long way from Lori Fielding to Laura Kincaid, too.

She had been a kid herself when she had married Buddy Fielding, Laura thought, nineteen and a little afraid of this hearing world where she was expected to function. Buddy had been her protector. For a while anyway. He'd liked to call her Lori, and would tell her to leave everything to him, he'd take care of her. Though at the time, she hadn't been sure that's what she wanted, she felt she had little choice since she dropped out of college when they'd decided to get married.

Soon, Buddy got grandiose ideas about a school for the deaf bearing his name. Laura accompanied him on fund-raising trips, hating every minute of Buddy's increasingly insincere posturing and flattering to get money from someone. Even after the school had been built, Buddy wasn't satisfied. Next, he built a big house with a swimming pool. When Laura asked him where they'd gotten the money for that, he had told her not to worry about unimportant details, that eventually the house would become the main office for the Fielding School for the Deaf and that the kids would use the pool. But that day didn't come.

Buddy began to look at Laura with new eyes, and suddenly he didn't want her to wear her hearing aid in public. He complained that it was ugly and that he didn't want it seen. He had said things about Laura that still stung.

Buddy's undoing was his decision to run for the city council. He dragged Laura to press conferences and rallies, always putting her forward and extolling the school and how he had been inspired by his deaf wife. Before it was over Laura felt that the sum total of her existence as a woman was reduced to a pair of ears that no longer functioned.

Buddy and Laura were on a fund-raising trip to Mexico when their world finally toppled. An investor in the school, seeing reports in the newspaper about Buddy's campaign and luxurious lifestyle, began asking questions.

After that came the investigations, the discovery of Buddy's creative bookkeeping and self-serving misappropriation of funds. Then came the public disgrace. The Fielding School for the Deaf was closed amid public clamor, and Laura still cringed when she remembered the ghastly press conference when it became clear that, not only had Buddy betrayed the school, but he'd betrayed Laura's trust as well. Buddy was forced to withdraw from the city council race because of his misdoings; the name Fielding was now synonymous with corruption.

Buddy left her that very night, his legacy of bitter words all that remained. Laura filed for divorce and assumed her maiden name. She dropped from sight, shunning interviews, and went back to school to study photography, something she'd taken up to fill the lonely hours when Buddy had been off somewhere.

A new director, Anne Tyler, was appointed at the re-named Hastings Institute, and she contacted Laura, telling her how fond the children were of her and asking her to continue her involvement with the school. Laura agreed, because she truly loved the children; now she volunteered there several times a week.

The children. Laura smiled down at the photographs. She was happy working here at *Springfield Today* and spending her free time at the Hastings Institute. She didn't need anything else in her life.

But even as she thought it, an image of blue eyes and a smiling mouth rose before her. *No.* She didn't need a man in her life.

It was six o'clock when Laura looked up sensing that someone was standing in front of her desk. Other female antennae were apparently at work too, as Katrina took time from her phone calls to advertisers to scoot over to Laura's desk and sidle up to David Evers. "Can I help you?" she purred, smiling a smile Laura hadn't seen since Katrina had landed a big bagel chain for a series of expensive ads.

David smiled politely. "Thank you, but I'm here to see Laura." Laura would have felt sorry for the disappointment on Katrina's face if she hadn't known that Katrina usually had five men on a figurative leash at any one time. Though Laura would bet that none was as attractive as David Evers. She felt a tinge of proprietary pride and immediately stifled it.

"Are you ready?" he asked, and she noticed that he made sure she was looking at him before he spoke.

Laura nodded. He helped her on with her long gray winter coat, and she tied a pale blue scarf over her hair. Laura carefully avoided looking at him as they stepped out into the January cold, not wanting him to feel he had to talk. A gust of wind bit into her neck as he took her arm and guided her toward a slightly rusted, very old, red compact car at the curb. She felt shy suddenly, as if she were a schoolgirl on her first date. She glanced at him and found his blue eyes studying her face. A rush of sweet warmth suffused her body, and unexpected desire flooded her like a dam breaking. Damn his gorgeous eyes anyway, she thought. She was *not* going to let herself get involved with a politician, not even if his eyes were sexier than Paul Newman's. She looked away, and he helped her into the car.

She kept her eyes averted during the car ride, and he touched her arm once to point out a flock of geese, their elongated forms dark against the gray sky. She nodded and smiled, swallowing down the rush of heat that coursed through her at his touch. A few random snowflakes blew past the window and she concentrated on them.

The restaurant he chose was a surprise to her — a large ice cream parlor that served light dinners as well. She was grateful that the place was well lit after the dates she'd endured in the dark, intimate four-star gourmet palaces where she could barely read the menu by the light of the mini-watt candles, much less her date's lips.

Laura's eyes lingered over the three-page

menu devoted to the ice cream dishes, hastily perusing the single page of main course options. He touched her hand, and she looked up to find him smiling at her. "Anything look good to you?" he asked.

Laura nodded. "Everything." She saw his face light up with a grin, and her heart started doing strange things again, things you normally associated with circuses and high-wire acts.

"Now this is what I had in mind," he said, leaning toward her conspiratorially. "What do you say to two hamburgers with chili sauce and then" — he waggled his eyebrows in enticement — "two of those jumbo sundaes with hot fudge sauce, peanuts, whipped cream, and the chocolate shavings on top?"

"The Turtle Supreme?" she said in awe.

"Come on, Ms. Kincaid. A hardworking lady like yourself? You can handle it." He glanced down at the menu and then back at her with a sly grin. "And if you can't, I'll help."

"Mr. Evers," she said lightly, "I don't believe you know who it is you're dealing with. I once won an ice-cream-eating contest."

"No," he said, teasing her, the grin broadening.

"Oh, yes. Three pints in fifteen minutes. I had a headache you wouldn't believe."

He laughed, and she let her gaze rove upward to his eyes, liking the way they darkened when he laughed. "What do you say," he began, leaning toward her again with a devilish smile, "we just skip the main course and go right to the ice cream?"

"I think I can handle that," she said, and his grin broadened.

The waitress came to their table then, and Laura watched her from the corner of her eye, noting how she angled her body toward David, her smile a bit too warm to be just politeness. The smile wasn't nearly as warm when the girl scooped up the menus and glanced at Laura, and Laura saw the frank envy there a second before the waitress's eyes slid to the small instrument in Laura's ear. Then came the expression all too familiar to Laura — shock and discomfort. "Anything else?" the waitress asked, her voice raised as she mouthed the words slowly. From the corner of her eye Laura saw two people at the next table turn to look.

"No, thank you," Laura said, quickly looking away but not in time to miss the waitress's renewed confidence as she smiled at David again.

Laura caught a glimpse of David's mouth moving and looked at him quickly. "I'm sorry," she said. "What?"

"I said I ordered us both iced tea. I hope that's okay."

She nodded, feeling a pang of something akin to sadness. It was strange, she thought, that emotions she hadn't felt in a long time were surfacing because of this man.

"They have good iced tea here," he said, his eyes on her face, his expression one she couldn't quite read. "Something herbal. And they put a hard peppermint candy in it too. It's different . . ." He looked away from her, frowning, and when he looked back she was struck by the hesitation on his face. "I'm sorry," he said.

"Sorry?" She didn't understand.

He shrugged. "Sorry that I'm babbling about iced tea when you probably don't give a damn. Sorry I didn't take you to a nicer place . . . Sorry about that waitress."

Laura watched him in bemusement. He seemed like a nice man. And that surprised her.

Laura smiled haltingly. "Iced tea is interesting," she said. "And I like this place." She took a deep breath. "And that waitress can go to hell."

He grinned, and Laura let herself look in his eyes again, a dangerous endeavor given the way her pulse took off erratically.

Laura pointedly avoided looking at the waitress when their ice cream concoctions came, and when she finally glanced up she found David studying her. "This is delicious," she said around a bite of chocolate sauce.

He nodded, but she could see that his mind wasn't on the food. "Ms. Kincaid," he began, setting down his spoon. "How bad is your hearing loss?"

Here it was, she thought ruefully, the million-dollar question that had sent more than one man scurrying out of her life.

"Profound," she said simply, using the word she had first heard from the otologist. "I have severe nerve damage. Hearing is nonexistent in my left ear and almost nonexistent in my right. But that *almost* is what lets me wear a hearing aid."

"So the hearing aid helps?" he asked.

Laura met his gaze levelly. "I can pick out a word now and then," she said evenly. "Others are badly distorted — it depends on the frequency — and then there is the vast majority which I can't hear at all. I lipread pretty well."

She wondered suddenly what he was thinking. What did any man think when she eventually told him the extent of her hearing loss? She steeled herself for whatever this man would feel. Pity? Condescension? Maybe even disdain because she wasn't in perfect working order? She'd seen all those looks before.

"And here I thought it was my riveting charm that kept your eyes on my face," he said, smiling with a certain degree of self-deprecation.

Laura relaxed and smiled back. Something she couldn't quite define was growing inside her, a feeling . . . She was liking this David Evers more and more, and she wasn't sure she wanted to.

"You speak very well," he said.

"Thank you. I've worked hard with a speech therapist. I was six when I lost my hearing — I had meningitis — so I was luckier than some. It's hard to learn to speak if you've never heard speech."

She was so matter-of-fact about it, he thought, watching her from across the table. And still, there was a wariness in her eyes, as though she didn't quite trust him, a stranger. Laura Kincaid was an odd mixture of assurance and tentative shyness, and he found himself drawn to her despite her obvious reticence. It was a long time since he'd enjoyed a leisurely dinner with a woman, and he found himself trying to prolong this one, asking Laura about her work at *Springfield Today* and her family. *No family,* she told him, and he caught that undercurrent of hesitation again. That's too bad, he told her, thinking how the hell does she do it on her own? He brought himself up short a moment later, realizing he'd been idly entertaining the thought that his two daughters would like Laura. A foolish thought from a foolish man, he chided himself. He had a political campaign to run, a newspaper to manage, two children to rear — he didn't need involvement with a woman now. And yet, that cold, blank place inside him was warmed by this woman.

He found himself watching her all through the meal, more puzzled by his own reaction to her than by her increasing silence. She looked almost like a woman with secrets, but he attributed that to the inner strength she must require to deal with a hearing world. She was coping in a world not her own, and he felt growing respect for her.

She found herself wondering what he was like in front of a television camera when he was being interviewed about his campaign. Somehow she couldn't picture him with the arrogant, superior smile that had been Buddy's trademark.

She glanced quickly at David, realizing she had been lost in her own thoughts, and found his eyes fixed on her. A fleeting look crossed his face, the look a stranger sometimes gives you on a bus or train — *yes, I know,* that look says — and she felt her throat constrict.

"Ms. Kincaid — Laura," he said, eyeing her steadily. "I would really like you to be the one to photograph my house. Beth told me you're the best photographer on staff, and I have a feeling she's already approached you about this. My home is very important to me, and I want the right person to capture it on film."

She watched him, frowning, then looked down at the table. "I don't know," she said hesitantly. It was David Evers's very attractiveness that was making her hedge. If she had taken an instant dislike to him she could have done the job with no qualms. But, he was stirring up thoughts and feelings inside her, things better left untouched . . .

"We'll leave it at that for now," he said at last, looking into her eyes until she met his gaze. His pensiveness faded a moment later. "Are you done?" he asked, smiling at the remains of her Turtle Supreme, and she let out a sigh of pure pigged-out satisfaction.

"It was the best meal I've had in a long time," she said honestly.

"Good." David was smiling at her, and she

looked away, pretending to hunt for her purse, because his eyes were making her pulse race uncontrollably again. "I guess we should go then," he said when she looked up. Laura saw reluctance on his face.

She told him where she lived, and they rode to the apartment in silence. There was still traffic on the Springfield streets, but it was thinning out, and David maneuvered the car easily. Night had fallen like a curtain, ushering in the kind of gray, bleak cold that made winter seem like forever. Laura stared out the window, relieved that he didn't want to talk. She was feeling unsettled, as if she'd expected this meeting to resolve something in her mind, but it hadn't.

He helped her out of the car when they got there and accompanied her inside. "Thank you," she said stiffly as he followed her onto the elevator. "I had a good time." She hunted in her purse for her key, and he touched her arm lightly.

"What floor?" he asked when she looked at him.

Laura felt herself flushing. He rattled her, and she didn't understand why. "Fourth."

He was at her side again as the elevator doors opened, and she walked quickly to her door. The clicking of her shoes on the wood hall was almost indiscernible to her, even with her hearing aid, and she thought again how different her world was from David Evers's.

A sad-eyed golden retriever bounded toward

them when the door opened, then stopped when it spotted David. Laura was crooning to the dog. "Hello, Horton," she said softly. "Did you miss me?"

After accepting Laura's petting, Horton turned to the serious business of inspecting David, taking a dignified sniff of his shoes before wagging his tail and allowing David to pet his head. The dog turned to follow Laura to the closet, and David smiled, thinking how much the dog resembled a stiff-lipped, solemn butler.

He remained standing in the doorway, his hands in his pockets, and when Laura turned uncertainly he said, "How did he get the name Horton?"

"From the Dr. Seuss book *Horton Hears a Who*. He's my set of ears. He's trained to come get me if the phone rings or someone rings the doorbell or if the smoke alarm goes off." She bent down to pat the dog, who was looking up at her in devotion.

Such simple everyday things, he thought, and she can't hear them. "Can't you get a louder doorbell?" he asked.

"I take off my hearing aid at night," she went on matter-of-factly, "and then there's the problem of recruitment. An ordinary but loud sound can be painfully loud for someone with a hearing aid. I used to have some trouble with the piercing noises, so my aid's adjusted lower for them."

He realized she was watching him uncertainly, and now she stepped toward him and made an aborted gesture. "May I take your coat?" she said. He saw that she really didn't want him to stay, though, so he smiled and shook his head.

"No, I ought to get home." They both stood there, only two feet apart, another long minute, and then David did something that surprised him. He put both hands on her arms and gently tugged her closer to him. Her eyes were on his face, such a silky shade of hazel and so wide — he tilted her chin up to him. Her mouth parted slightly in a breathless *oh* and David felt such an ache inside that he nearly groaned. She was so beautiful and so vulnerable and he shouldn't be doing this . . .

Laura was surprised when his head lowered to hers and she stood stiffly, not sure at first what was happening. Then his lips brushed hers, and she clutched at his arms to keep from losing her balance. Such sweetness in his mouth, in his hesitation. A tenderness she wanted to trust. It had been so long since a man had kissed her, and abstinence had done nothing to mitigate the need for a man's touch. Against all reason, she leaned into his embrace and felt his lips move more urgently over hers. Fire burst in her veins, and she savored the feel of his mouth, clean and hard, against her lips and then her cheek. His fingers moved up to cradle her face, stroking softly into her hair, and she sighed heavily as he continued to kiss her jaw and then her temple. His breath was uneven against her skin.

When David pulled away, his eyes were bright

with wanting her; they caught her gaze and held.

Laura ached with burgeoning desire, her pulse pounding just from the look on his face. But she let her arms fall to her sides. She'd had a lover once before, and she still stung from his criticism. *"No man wants to make love to a woman who can't understand a damn thing he says unless she's staring at his face,"* Buddy had complained the night he'd left her bed for good. No, she wouldn't take another man into her bed. Buddy had brought heartache enough.

Slowly his hands left her face, and she could have cried with wanting him to touch her again. "Good night," he said, taking a step backward. Laura couldn't seem to make her mouth work, and just stared at him foolishly. A moment later he was gone. Laura had never felt so lonely in her whole life.

Chapter 2

She had dreamed about him. When she woke up
Saturday morning the details of the dream were
hazy, but she knew it had been about him. *His
hands.* That's what she had dreamed, Laura realized as she washed her face. She flushed as she
remembered just where his hands had touched
her.

It was odd, but she had dreamed about his
voice, too. Of course, she hadn't really heard
more than an occasional rumble like distant
thunder. But in her dream his voice was deep
and caressing. In her dream she had been lying
in a field of grass, surrounded by profound silence. A breeze wafted over her, but she could
hear nothing, could just feel it and see the grass
moving in rhythm. And then David had appeared beside her, and he had started touching
her with his hands. She closed her eyes and,
strangely enough, she could hear his voice then,
strong and clear and resonant like a bell. She
couldn't understand what he was saying, but his
tone was melodic and soothing, like songs she
remembered hearing so long ago.

Laura shook her head to clear it of the dream
and began to dress, putting on black cords and a

powder blue pullover. She fitted the earpiece into her ear, then shook her hair so that it fell softly about her shoulders. She turned on the hearing aid and frowned. It had always been a little jarring to her to hear sounds again in the morning after a night of deep silence, but lately there was not as much difference as in the past. She turned up the gain control until she heard a faint buzzing and crooned to Horton, who had followed her from bed to bathroom and back again. "Breakfast time, buddy?" she asked, stroking his broad head. She glanced at the calendar in the kitchen as she went to the cupboard and checked the date for her appointment with the otologist next month. She'd have to ask if her aid needed adjustment.

She was watching Horton eat, a smile teasing the corner of her mouth at his always ravenous appetite, when he lifted his head, ears cocked, and began to bark. He bounced up and down in front of her, lifting one paw, and she knew that either the phone had rung or someone was at the door.

It was the door, she saw by the light blinking to the left of the doorjamb. It was one of the little extras she'd installed in the apartment shortly after moving in. When she opened the door there was David Evers.

"Hi," he said awkwardly, giving a little lift of his shoulders as if he was as bewildered as she to find himself on the other side of her door. He was wearing a brown leather jacket and crisp charcoal slacks, and with his windblown hair and dancing eyes he looked devastating.

"Come in," she said faintly.

"You're probably wondering what I'm doing here on a Saturday morning," he said after a long silence while she tried to stop admiring his good looks. She had the feeling that if she tried to walk now her knees would refuse to cooperate. Her eyes fell to the box cradled beneath his arm and then looked back at his face quizzically.

"This is for you," he said, pulling out the box and handing it to her, and she saw that it was only one of two.

She looked at the box in her hands and then back to his eyes, which hadn't left her face. "Dog biscuits. Just what I always wanted," she said in bemusement.

David frowned and tore his eyes from her face to inspect the box. "No, no," he said impatiently. "These are for Horton. This is for you."

The second box, standard white bakery cardboard, was tied with string. An interesting aroma was issuing from the inside. "My, my," she said. "And what have we here? Isn't it too early in the day for this?"

His mouth crooked up in a devilish smile, that look she was beginning to like so much. "My grandmother's bourbon pound cake," he said. "She runs a little bakery. Won't retire. This is one of her specialties."

They looked at each other awkwardly a minute longer and Laura felt that same bone-melting reaction to him. She had to do something before she started babbling like an idiot. "I put some coffee on . . ." she managed to get out. "May I take your jacket?" She hung the jacket in the closet, turning away from his mesmerizing face and starting for the kitchen before she lost her composure. What was he doing here?

He'd trusted his instincts to know what to do once he got here, but so far David was at a loss. She seemed glad to see him — in a surprised sort of way, he amended wryly. A minute later she had poured them each a cup of coffee, and they settled down at her kitchen table with the cake while Horton vigorously attacked the pile of dog biscuits on the floor.

Her kitchen was nice. Bright yellow flowered wallpaper and white percale curtains made it look sunny and inviting. The kitchen table was in front of a window overlooking a tree-lined street, and he saw two kids kicking a soccer ball back and forth on the walk, their shouts ringing in the air. Their breath came in frosty bursts as they ran back and forth.

"You kids keep it down out there!" a woman bellowed from a window near the street. "Your father's trying to sleep. And put on your hat. It's twenty degrees, for crying out loud!"

David grinned at Laura. "Is that the resident weather lady?"

She looked at him blankly and then glanced out the window. When she turned her eyes to his face again he saw no comprehension there. She

37

hadn't heard anything that was going on outside.

"I'm sorry," he said, his smile fading. "A woman was shouting at those boys."

"Mrs. Gibbons, no doubt," she said, looking out the window again, frowning. "Let me get you some more coffee."

He still had half a cup, and he watched her covertly as she stepped behind the counter. She seemed to be adjusting something, and he guessed it was the controls to her hearing aid. He'd called a doctor friend of his last night and asked some questions about hearing loss, and he now knew enough to figure that Laura wore a compact aid containing a microphone, small and sophisticated, yet still limited. He also knew that she had minimized the severity of her hearing loss for him. "That's rough," his friend had said on the phone when David described Laura's situation. "She probably has a devil of a time."

He decided that if he was to learn to know this woman better, then he would have to be forthright. There was no point in either of them ignoring her difference. He got up from the table and went to her, gently touching her shoulder. She turned with a little start, her eyes shadowed with frustration. "Are you having trouble with your hearing aid?" he asked.

"I think the battery might be bad," she said hesitantly, her eyes searching his face.

"Let's have a look."

She turned away a bit, reaching into her ear to dislodge the aid. David pretended not to notice that her fingers were trembling as she turned back to him, the small battery in her palm.

He took it from her, letting his fingers linger just a fraction longer than need be. Her skin was soft and warm, and he felt his heart begin a steady, drumming beat. "This should last a good long time. Do you have some new ones?"

She went to a kitchen drawer and returned with a new pack. He opened it for her and put the new battery in the delicate unit. He watched as she adjusted the controls.

"Testing, one, two, three," she said lightly, her eyes meeting his, then sliding away. She began adjusting the aid, and he saw that her fingers were trembling again. She chewed her lip as she struggled with the placement, finally flushing as she glanced up at him again.

"Let me help," he said quietly, nodding when she seemed about to refuse.

"I can't . . ." she began, flustered.

"Don't worry," he assured her. "It's okay."

She smiled a bit, and he found his own fingers shaky as they slid over hers. She was trying to angle it just right, but her trembling fingers failed to restrain her cascading hair. Not daring to meet her eyes, David eased the silken mass away from her ear. In a second, the aid was secured in place. He looked at her face then and found her enormous hazel eyes fixed on him. "Thank you," she said in a small voice.

"I have sisters," he told her, his hands reluctantly leaving her. "You might say I have experience in the field." She smiled but didn't say anything, and he suddenly found his hands cupping her face.

She stood very still, watching him the way a fawn watches a human interloper in the forest, and his breath caught in his throat at the raw vulnerability on her face. He brought his mouth down to hers in excruciating slowness, and when his lips found their objective he kissed her like a man slaking a long, burning thirst.

The hearing aid was uncomfortable against the pressure of his hand, but Laura didn't care. All that mattered right now was the sweet, hard feel of his mouth on hers. His hands moved restlessly over her ribs, coming to rest with his thumbs just barely touching the beginning swell of her breasts. She wanted his touch there, too, and strained her body toward him. It had been so long . . .

He lifted his mouth a fraction and her head fell back languidly, her long hair hanging to the counter. She felt rather than heard the muffled crash behind her, registering some *thud* through vibrations. He pulled back, the spell broken. She could see a surprised intensity on his face before his eyes left hers and moved to the counter.

Her head swung up, and she flushed, feeling as abandoned as she had when she first lost her hearing, when, despite her mother's comforting, she knew she'd never truly hear music again, or the voices of her friends. She hadn't even wanted a hearing aid at first, but her mother had prevailed. "You'll at least hear a little *something*," she'd told Laura. "Remember that — something is better than nothing."

Sometimes over the years she'd wondered if that was really true.

David was picking up the framed photograph that had fallen facedown on the counter, studying it before he set it back. Laura glanced at the photo, her heart racing. It was such a part of her everyday life that she'd forgotten it was there. Three bright-eyed children, two boys and a girl, grinned at the camera, and on one was visible the cord running from his ear to the hearing aid inside his shirt pocket. They were students at the Hastings Institute. And Laura seldom mentioned the Hastings Institute to anyone she didn't know well. Lori Fielding seemed like a distant memory, a bad dream, and Laura steadfastly refused to open up that part of her past for anyone.

"Nice-looking kids," David said, looking at her quizzically.

"They're . . . cousins," she said lamely, remembering too late that she'd already told him she had no family. "Distant cousins," she amended, cursing herself for her foolish lie. Of course he wouldn't believe that.

He studied the picture a moment longer, then looked into her face again. "I want you to see my house," he said. And there was something in his expression that told her he didn't often extend that invitation.

41

Laura knew that this was where she should turn back. If she went with David she was committing herself to taking the photographs, and they both knew it. It was an irrevocable step. She had fought long and hard to become what she was today. She had struggled to get an education: to learn to lipread, and sign when need be; to learn a vocation, photography; and to get a job to support herself. None of the steps had been easy and all had been accomplished on her own. The product of a hasty marriage between two people singularly unsuited to each other, Laura had not missed the father who was on the road putting together ill-fated business deals more than he was home. And when her parents divorced she had felt no loss of security, because she had her mother. It was Laura's mother who nursed her through the meningitis and who prodded her to claim what avenues of communication were left to her after she lost her hearing. "Slow progressive nerve loss," the doctor had said. "We don't know where it will end." And Laura had nearly given up. But not her mother. She spent hours patiently sitting facing Laura, speaking slowly and deliberately until Laura began to learn to lipread. And when Laura totally lost hearing in her left ear in high school, it was her mother who held her and soothed her while she cried hot, bitter tears. No, Emily Kincaid would never let Laura give up on anything. And when her mother died, Laura had felt that loss more keenly than anything in her life.

She searched David's face now, looking for something, though she wasn't even sure what it was. She shouldn't go. She knew she was getting in deeper than she'd intended with this man, and she admitted that it scared her. She had had a lot of disappointments with men. But when she looked into his eyes she saw . . . *something.* Something that reminded her of her mother's words. *You cheat yourself by not trying, Laura, not by failing.*

"I have to walk Horton first," she said.

His face relaxed at her acquiescence, and his smile made her knees tremble again. "Why don't you bring him with us? I have enough room there for him to run if he wants."

So Horton clambered into the back seat, and Laura laughed as he tried to lean over the front and get a healthy sniff of the piece of bourbon cake she was munching. She finally relented and gave him a small piece, and he licked his lips in satisfaction.

"Don't tell your grandmother," Laura said. "She'd probably be horrified to know I squandered even one little piece of that wonderful cake."

"Don't worry," he said wryly. "She's a pushover for dogs. He'd probably get his own cake."

Laura noticed that when he was driving he always turned his head partly toward her when he spoke, so she could understand what he was saying. She liked the way his eyes caught hers and seemed to smile when he talked. Unconsciously she had angled her body slightly toward him, so her hearing aid was positioned that much more in his direction. She ought to get the hearing aid checked, she thought in annoyance. It didn't seem to be picking things up very well.

"It must be nice coming from a big family," she said a trifle wistfully. "Sisters and a grandmother."

"A brother, too," he told her with a sideways smile. "I'm the oldest of four. As such, I'm known as the bossy one. My youngest sister, Erin, says I was a royal pain growing up. Always making her redo her math homework." He gave her an engaging grin. "My grandmother ran herd on all of us."

"Your parents?" she asked hesitantly.

"They divorced shortly after Erin was born. Both remarried and . . . well, sort of left us in the care of Grendel."

"Grendel?" she repeated, not sure she'd gotten the name right from his lip movements.

He nodded, smiling, and she noted that talking about his grandmother and brother and sisters brought an easy warmth to his face. "That was Erin's doing. She couldn't say Grandmother Wendell — that was my mother's maiden name — when she was a baby, and it sort of came out Grendel."

"It sounds like something you'd call a big bear," Laura said, and he laughed again.

"You'll see how well it suits her when you meet her," he promised, and Laura found herself worrying as she covertly studied his stark profile. She wasn't at all sure she was ready to meet his family, to accept the easy familiarity he was offering. Was that really it? Familiarity? She could read other things in his eyes, a gentle brooding when they took on a grayish cast, a lonely need when they were blue. And Laura was well aware that some men didn't consider her the proper kind of woman to fill a man's needs. She felt a chill at the prospect of meeting his family and averted her eyes to stare out the window.

They were driving out of the city. Condominiums, retirement homes, and corporate offices dotted the highway, all with clean, opaque windows as gray and smooth as the January sky. The wind buffeted the car, and she frowned as she remembered something that had bothered her since yesterday. What was a man who owned a Frank Lloyd Wright house doing driving a rattletrap like this? She glanced around the front seat of the car and saw that the interior was nearly as abused as the exterior. Foam padding poked through two holes in the upholstery, and the floor mats were covered with a thin layer of dust and gravel. The glove compartment lock was missing, leaving a gaping hole and leading Laura to wonder how one opened it. Animal hairs sifted through the gray light from the windows, landing on the upholstery where they joined more of their kind.

"Do you have pets?" Laura asked cautiously,

looking at him again.

"Is there a problem with Horton?" he asked. "I mean, he doesn't eat cats or anything, does he?"

"Heavens no. In fact, I think he's a little scared of them."

She watched David curiously when he didn't say anything else, finding it hard to picture him with a troop of cats in his Frank Lloyd Wright house. Her fingers strayed to a hole in the seat, her finger idly plucking at the torn fabric.

"I should have brought the other car," he said suddenly, casting her a worried look, as if his mode of transportation had just struck him as not refined enough for her.

"No, it's all right," she assured him. "This is fine."

"Grendel has the other car today," he said. "She had two wedding cakes to be delivered and set up at the same time and only one delivery truck. And my brother Alan borrowed my truck to go to an auction. He had his eye on a grandfather's clock."

"No, really. This is okay." Her errant finger came away with a hefty piece of padding snagged on it, and Laura, disconcerted, tried to stuff it back in place. Lord, this car was a mess!

When she looked back at him he was laughing. "Grendel thinks this car is a disgrace," he said, still chuckling. "And she's probably right. But it's useful. And I can't bring myself to get rid of something I've had so long." He raised his brows and told her with mock importance, "I took my date to the prom in this car."

"I think she left her corsage here," Laura said with wry levity as she disentangled a dried flower petal from a spring protruding from the back of the seat.

"That must belong to Mary," he said, laughing. "I took her to the florist yesterday and she bought a plant."

He didn't elaborate, leaving Laura to wonder who Mary was. She tried to determine what he was thinking by studying his face, but he was looking straight ahead now, small lines furrowing the corners of his eyes. He was thinking of something else, she realized. Of Mary, perhaps? Laura turned away, unsure of what she should say.

She had looked so familiar for an instant, David thought, frowning as he turned the car off the exit ramp. Something about Laura had deviled him since he first saw her, and a moment ago, with that slightly surprised look in her eyes, some half-forgotten, ghostly image had risen tantalizingly close to consciousness. But he couldn't quite grasp it, and it slid away.

He turned the car onto a long, tree-lined residential street, and from the corner of his eye he saw her straighten up and peer out the window in interest. He liked the way her emotions shone through her eyes, making the hazel sparkle like burnished copper when something caught her fancy. The homes on this street were all enormous and old, and he drove slowly, enjoying stealing sideways glances of her. She was absorbed in the houses — he could see the intensity lighting up her face — and he was getting a lot of pleasure from watching her. He could still smell the clean, sweet scent he'd caught of her shampoo when he'd kissed her in her kitchen, and his fingers tingled with the memory of her soft skin. She was invading his waking and sleeping moments the way no woman had since Barbara, and he was feeling unsettled.

He slowed the car and maneuvered it into a blacktop drive that led through a wrought iron gate.

"This is where you live?" she asked as he followed the curve of the drive and the house came into view.

He nodded, easing the car forward. "It's not what you expected?" he asked.

She shook her head. "No . . . it's so *big*. I've seen Frank Lloyd Wright houses before, but I never really pictured anyone living in them."

In her words he heard her hesitation, her sudden withdrawal, and he realized he should have prepared her better. Of course this wasn't what she expected after he picked her up in this car. He should have told her. But told her what? That his house was huge? That it was important to him that she see it and yet he didn't fully understand why? Nothing he was doing seemed to make sense. It was just that when he kissed her, he had felt right and alive for the first time in so long.

He stopped the car in front of the house and sat silently, watching her take in the details. The house was masonry with wood and brick accents, and the whole was like a living being in its complexity. The house could have been woven rather than built. It was a multitude of layered flat planes, and Laura's photographer's eye was already delighting in the possibilities. The various wings of the house intersected each other at right angles while wooden cantilevers and nearly flat roofs that extended well beyond the walls cast subtle shadows and gave an airy appearance, as if the house were only a mirage and might float away at any time. Up one step from the drive, a tiled patio led toward the arched doorway, which was nearly hidden in the folds of angled walls. A low stone wall surrounded the patio, punctuated here and there by a giant stone planter filled with trailing ivy, now denuded of its leaves.

"It's magnificent," Laura murmured, not even sure if she'd spoken. She glanced at his face and realized she must have, because he was nodding, a contemplative look on his face.

"It's been in Barbara's family since the time of her grandparents," he said, not looking at Laura, and she strained to watch his mouth. "Her parents lived here, and then when they died unexpectedly the house came to us." He fell silent, frowning, and Laura discovered that her heart was hammering against her ribs, robbing her breath. He was married?

He glanced at her finally and, seeing her trying to watch his mouth, quickly said, "I'm sorry. I didn't mean to turn away while I was talking." She could see that his eyes were gray now and as bleak as the January sky. "Barbara was my wife," he said simply. He opened the door and got out, leaning in again to lever the driver's seat forward and call Horton. "He can run around here," he told Laura as he opened her door. "The whole place is fenced."

An ecstatic Horton went snuffing along the grass at the wall, and Laura turned back to the house to see two girls, who looked to be about thirteen and seven, coming toward them. The girls, in denim jeans and jackets, had stylish layered blond hair, which blew back to reveal gold hoop earrings. The older of the two led the way, the one behind more or less imitating her sister's actions — they had to be sisters from the looks of it. Focusing on the lead girl's lips, Laura could make out what she was saying.

"Grendel won't let me wear these earrings to the party tonight. She says they're cheap looking. God, Dad, *everybody* wears earrings like these." The older girl's lips closed in a petulant bow.

Laura was startled to hear her call David "Dad," although it had already dimly registered that these two must be his daughters. She glanced at David and found him eyeing the girls with a frown.

"First, those earrings are definitely too gaudy

for the party, and second, we have company."

Their grievance aired, if not resolved to their satisfaction, the girls curiously turned their attention to Laura. "Laura Kincaid," David said, stepping forward so she could see his mouth better. "These are my daughters, Mary and Jean. Girls, Laura might be photographing the house for *Springfield Today*."

The older one, the one he'd called "Mary," brightened. "Oh, too much. Do you really work for a magazine? Do you get to go to neat places?"

Before Laura could answer, Mary turned to Jean, and Laura couldn't see either of their faces to guess what they were saying. Mary turned back with an expectant expression, saying, "What's his name?"

"I'm sorry," Laura said, having no idea what she was talking about. "I wear a hearing aid and I can't understand what you're saying unless I can see your mouth."

Mary looked taken aback, but Jean peered around her sister, smiling up at Laura and obviously trying to get a better look at the hearing aid. "What's your dog's name?" Jean asked, nodding toward Horton.

"Horton," Laura said. "And he loves to be scratched behind his ears."

"Let's go inside," David said as Jean rushed to greet Horton, who was wagging his tail expectantly. "It's not polite to keep our guest outside in this cold."

He looped his arm around Laura's shoulders,

and she gave him a hesitant smile. He'd certainly sprung enough surprises on her for one day.

But one more surprise waited in the interior of the enormous house. A tiny, stately woman with short, curly white hair bustled toward them as they entered the massive tiled foyer. She looked to be about eighty, but her jaunty carriage belied that age. She had large dribbles of some kind of red sauce down her pink sweater, and she was wiping her hands on her jeans. Laura knew before she spoke that this was the formidable Grendel.

"Ah, you must be Laura," the woman said, smiling broadly and extending a hand, which Laura shook. "I'm David's grandmother, Olivia Wendell, but no one calls me anything but 'Grendel' anymore." She turned as the girls entered, and before Laura could answer she said, "Good God! Will you two take off those disgusting earrings! And comb your hair before you come down to lunch."

Mary rolled her eyes, but she and Jean dutifully headed for the wooden staircase off the foyer. Mary turned around at the steps. "Don't talk with your back to her," she informed Grendel importantly. "She wears a hearing aid."

Laura suppressed a smile as Grendel, without turning around to the girls, closed her eyes at this supreme straining of her patience, and said, "I *know* that, Mary." She turned her attention back to David. "Go show Laura around the house and we'll have some brunch when you get done." Laura realized with a start that David had prepared Grendel for her visit.

"Did you get your cakes delivered and set up?" David asked.

"No problem," Grendel said.

David nodded and steered Laura down the foyer toward the rest of the house. If she thought it was huge from the outside, it seemed even more mammoth inside. The living room in particular intrigued her, and she mentally calculated what angles she would try to capture on film. The floor was wood, and the fireplace was stone, and then there was the ceiling — a series of pentagonally shaped glass panels, actually lights intersected with wooden beams, and the effect was stunning.

"Come on," David said, touching her arm to get her attention. "There's lots more to see, and Grendel will holler at me if I let her brunch get cold."

The house was so huge that Laura wondered if they would finish the tour in time for dinner, much less brunch, but still she could hardly contain her excitement over the picture possibilities. The angles were fantastic and dramatic, and the rooms seemed to come alive.

She noted the homey, artistic touches in each room, the beautiful cross-stitched bedspread, a mass of pink roses in the guest bedroom. There were watercolors of Illinois landmarks on almost every wall, and a tablecloth in the dining room bore a delicate edging of needlework lilies. The theme was carried through in the garden outside the dining room window, where Laura could pick out the wintery shapes of rose bushes in neat patterns, and evergreens trimmed to compact symmetry.

It was a woman's touch she saw everywhere, and instinctively she knew it wasn't Grendel's. She turned from the window and traced a finger over the needlework bouquet of daisies hung on the wall. "Everything is so beautiful," she said without looking at him.

He touched her arm, and she turned to find him smiling faintly. "I can't talk to you when you won't look at me," he admonished her gently, and she realized that she had not wanted him to talk to her. She was in another woman's house, and it made her unsure and self-conscious around him.

"Barbara did that," he said, nodding toward the daisies. The lines deepened in his face as she saw his chest move in a silent sigh. "She died three years ago," he said, so softly that Laura strained to see each word on his lips. "Cancer."

"How awful for you," Laura said in quiet sympathy.

"It was hard on all of us. The girls especially. They each cope in their own way. You can see that Mary is the chatterbox, all animation, but that exterior hides a lot of hurt. And Jean was just a baby. She withdrew into a shell. Even now she's the silent one."

And you? Laura wondered silently.

"Barbara was an artist," David said, his eyes cloudy and gray as he gestured around the room. "She did almost all the watercolors you see, as well as all the needlework. She even designed needlework kits and sold them in craft stores in the area."

Laura found herself envying Barbara the life she must have had: loving husband, beautiful daughters, fulfilling work. "Tell me about her," she said softly, seeing the closeted feelings shadowing David's eyes.

He looked at Laura a moment before he spoke. "She made us a family," he said simply. "She filled this house with sound and laughter and good feelings." A smile barely touched the corners of his mouth. "And she kept us all on the straight and narrow," he said. "I remember when Mary came home from second grade, insisting her mother had to let her take one of her pictures to show the other kids because they wouldn't believe that Mary's mother was an artist. Then it came out that Mary had embellished the truth a bit and had told the kids that one of her mother's watercolors hung in the White House." David laughed at the memory, and Laura saw years fall away from his face. "I can still hear Mary. 'But, Mom, it's almost true. You sold one to the mayor, didn't you?' Barbara spent all afternoon convincing Mary that the mayor wasn't quite the same as the president. 'We won't have any varnishing of the truth,' Barbara said." David's voice quavered slightly, and his smile was sad. "That's what was special about her. She was the kind of woman who couldn't keep a secret. She had to buy Christmas presents on Christmas Eve so she wouldn't spill the beans and tell everyone what she'd gotten them." He laughed. "Every woman has her own beauty, and Barbara's was her innocence. She was that rare species — someone who was exactly what she appeared to be."

Laura stared out the window before she could look at him again. She didn't feel like that rare species herself, exactly what she appeared to be. She suddenly felt like Lori Fielding in another woman's house.

"Laura," David said suddenly, looking intently into her face. "I want you to do the photographs of the house. I think you can understand why," he hurried on when she would have interrupted him. "You bring something special back here, and we all need that badly. I'm not asking just for myself. This is for Grendel and the girls, too. Please." His hands came up and hesitated, then settled lightly on her shoulders, sending waves of feeling through her whole body.

She couldn't, she argued with herself as she stared back into his beseeching eyes. She was nothing like his wife. She wasn't innocent and she kept secrets.

But there was something here that she needed, too. And right now, with his hands gently touching her shoulders, that need overrode all reason and she found herself nodding yes.

"Good," he said softly, and the smile that touched his mouth opened up a door inside Laura, and she saw the loneliness she'd kept so carefully hidden.

Chapter 3

"Come on in here, Horton, and have some brunch," Jean said at the open door, and Laura held her breath. David had brought her to the kitchen just in time to read the invitation on Jean's lips, and she worried about Grendel's reception of a large, ungainly furball in her domain.

She needn't have worried. Grendel didn't even bat an eye. "I'm not setting a place at the table for him," she informed Jean. "He can eat from a paper plate on the floor."

"A paper plate?" Jean groaned in disgust.

"All right," Grendel said, apparently giving in. "Give him the stoneware — but *not* the china."

Laura gave David a quick glance and found him grinning. "Don't worry. They won't give him silverware."

Laura looked down as Jean touched her arm tentatively. "Grendel said to ask you if it's okay if Horton has brunch with us." There was breathless expectation in Jean's eyes, and Laura realized with a pang how important everything was to this little girl, and how devastating it must be to her not to remember her mother.

She smiled gratefully at Grendel over Jean's shoulder and said, "It's fine. Horton's off duty when he's not in the apartment with me."

"Off duty?" Jean said. "What's that?"

"In the apartment, he's my good set of ears," Laura explained. "It's his job to bark and come get me when the doorbell buzzes or the phone rings."

Jean thought about that a moment, then frowned. "But how can you talk on the phone if you can't hear?"

"I have a special machine attached to my phone that flashes a light to tell me in code what the other person is saying. Of course, the other person has to have a machine, too. My boss at work has one as well as —" Laura felt the blood pounding in her throat. "As well as some other friends," she finished lamely. She had almost said "as well as the Hastings Institute." She didn't feel comfortable yet sharing that part of her life.

"Oh," Jean said matter-of-factly. "Then we'd better get a machine too, hadn't we, Daddy?"

David was smiling when Laura looked at him. "I guess so, honey."

Grendel shooed everyone to the table, dishing a healthy portion of eggs Benedict onto Horton's stoneware plate before she placed the meal on the table. "See what I mean?" David said, elbowing Laura lightly. "Horton gets fed before we do."

"Now don't go picking on the poor dog," Grendel warned him. "He's very important to Laura, so he deserves to be treated well."

59

David's eyes were twinkling and his lips twitching, and Laura couldn't help smiling herself. Mary came into the kitchen nonchalantly, placing her hands on her hips as she surveyed the table. "Oh, gross!" she said. "Do we have to eat that?"

Grendel rolled her eyes. "There's cereal in the cupboard."

Mary shuffled her feet a bit and frowned. "Well, I guess I could force myself," she finally allowed, and Laura saw that behind the confident, brash exterior was a little girl who wasn't at all sure of herself. What a loss their mother's death must have been to them, she thought again.

Horton's ears went up as mewing issued from the hallway and two kittens came bouncing into the kitchen. The next minute he was cowering in the corner, his tail tucked between his legs. "Oh, Horton, you silly boy," Jean said, hurrying to him. Laura couldn't pick out the rest of the girl's one-sided dialogue with Horton, but soon he was licking her face and then tentatively sniffing the inquisitive kittens. Laura grinned at David. "I think she's found her calling. She'd make a great psychologist."

"Dr. Burnham said she's trying to mother everything since Mom died," Mary announced offhandedly, picking at her eggs.

Laura glanced at David and saw the weariness descend deep into his eyes until they were ashen. He exhaled painfully, like a swimmer too long under water. "Dr. Burnham is the psychologist who talked to the girls after . . . their mother died," he said slowly. "I didn't think I was doing a very good job of helping them."

Grendel shook her head, her eyes soft and luminous. "You were so tired, David. You and Barbara fought a long, hard battle. It took its toll."

Silence fell over the table, and Laura unconsciously sought out Jean's face. The girl was still bent over Horton, playing with him and the kittens, and though her lips moved, Laura couldn't hear what she was saying. She was off in a little world of her own, and Laura's heart went out to her.

It was Jean who broke the strange, uncomfortable spell that had fallen over the table. Rising from her position by Horton's side, she came to her chair and began to eat. "He'll be all right now," she told Laura across the table. "I told him that these cats won't bother him."

Laura felt David relax beside her, and she smiled, noting that Grendel's shoulders let themselves sink slightly. Horton followed Jean to the table and morosely laid his head on her lap. "We're friends," Jean told her great-grandmother.

"I can see that," Grendel said. "Now why don't you and your friend have some coffee cake, and then you can go outside again."

"I think I want to talk to Laura," Jean said. "Then we'll go out."

When brunch ended and Laura would have followed Grendel as she began clearing dishes, the older woman laid her hand on Laura's arm and said, "I don't need you right now. Why don't you stay with Jean for a while? David can help with the cleanup."

Laura watched David and Grendel disappear around the corner, where she had seen a small alcove with a dishwasher on her tour, and then she turned to Jean with a smile. "Well, it seems we escaped kitchen duty this time. What shall we do?"

Jean looked down at the floor, rubbing her shoe in a circle. "Do you want to see my stuffed animals?"

"That sounds nice," Laura said. "What about you, Mary?"

"I have to do a report on Lincoln," Mary said, rolling her eyes, "and Grendel and Dad said I can't go to the party until it's done."

"Well, good luck," Laura said.

"Thanks. Hey, sometime do you think I could come see your office? Just for a school report," she added hastily.

"Sure," Laura said. "Anytime." She hid her smile, remembering how hard it was to be a teenager, trying to remain poised and nonchalant on the surface, with all those wants and insecurities bubbling underneath.

Jean's room was as spacious as the other rooms in the house, but its profusion of windows surrounded by trees gave it the flavor of a hideaway, and Laura decided it suited the child perfectly. The stuffed animals covered the bed, and it was obvious that Jean had meticulously arranged them.

"Well, who do we have here?" Laura asked, lightly touching the fuzzy ear of a tiger with orange eyes.

"That's Judith," Jean said. "Grendel gave her to me one Christmas." She picked up a long, plush pink snake and giggled as she wrapped it around her neck. "And Daddy won this one for me at the church fair last year. He knocked over a bunch of cans with a baseball to get it."

"And who's this?" Laura asked, smiling as she picked up a small teddy bear whose one ear looked well chewed.

"That's Edmund," Jean said, and her face became serious. "My mom gave him to me, but I don't remember. He's lonesome for her and he feels bad because he doesn't remember her so well. But I tell him that's okay and he shouldn't worry."

Laura saw the pain in her face, the pain that was so big for a girl who was so small. And the space inside her that had opened up a crack at David's touch now opened wider for his two daughters.

When Laura and David stood at the door, their coats on, Horton wagging his tail between them, David grinned as he announced that Laura was going to photograph the house. The two girls beamed and squealed, although Mary made a valiant effort to remain unfazed. "That chills me out," she said, and from Mary's expression Laura assumed that being chilled out was good. Grendel hugged her impulsively, and Laura, to her surprise, found her eyes misting.

"We'll be so glad to see you again," Grendel said. Her voice was low, and Laura had to watch her mouth carefully to catch what she said. "Barbara loved this house so, and it was one of her last wishes that others get to see it too."

Again Laura reminded herself that this house and these people belonged to another woman, and they were still mourning her.

David put Horton in the back seat, then held Laura's door for her. She finally looked up from the seat when he didn't close the door and found him watching her, a warm half smile on his face. "They really liked you, you know," he said, the smile widening. "A lot."

Laura had felt that too, but although it warmed her it also made her sad. By no stretch of the imagination was she like Barbara, at least the way she was in David's memory, and Laura couldn't help thinking that Barbara had been sheltered. She felt her own marriage to Buddy Fielding and those awful days in the public eye after the Fielding School was closed had been some rite of passage for herself, so that her own innocence was long gone.

He touched her arm when they were out on the highway, and when she looked at him, her heart thudded in her throat. He was such a handsome man, his hair slightly windblown, his collar turned up at the neck, his eyes so intensely blue now, and an inviting expression playing around his mouth.

"Jean took her mother's death very hard," he said, his hand still on her arm though her eyes were riveted to his face. "She's a shy, lonely child. Today was the first time she's ever said more than three words to anyone other than Grendel, Mary, or me. Laura, I can't tell you how much that means to me."

"David," she began helplessly. "David, I was . . .." But she couldn't tell him, not when he was looking at her like this, seeing Laura Kincaid and not Lori Fielding. She couldn't tell him now. "I liked your family very much," she said softly, then turned her head to look out the window, feeling his fingers squeeze her arm gently before he let go.

He touched her shoulder after he'd walked her to her apartment door, and he was struck by the sadness in her face when she turned to him. "When will you start photographing?" he asked.

"I have to finish a few things for Beth at the office, but I should be ready tomorrow afternoon."

"Good." He nodded. "I have some work at the office myself, and I have to meet with a group of my campaign backers at noon, but I'll try to get away to meet you at the house."

"You don't have to do that," she said, absently reaching down to pet Horton, who was waiting patiently by her side.

"I know that, Laura," he said, wondering again what man had hurt her enough to cause this stubborn resistance in her, this refusal to let anyone know her easily. He wanted to kiss her again and feel that soft skin yield beneath him, but he didn't. He decided to give her some room instead. Gently brushing back her hair, he gave her a shadowy smile and said good-bye. And on the drive home he couldn't forget the shimmery hazel eyes that seemed so full of a yearning that Laura Kincaid wouldn't acknowledge.

Laura Kincaid. What was it that was so familiar about her? That haunted, lonely look she had when he'd left her had stayed with him, shoving at his memory but unable to break through.

He sat in his den in the dark maroon leather chair, leaning back and massaging his neck as he thought about Laura. Grendel poked her head in and came to the chair with a cup of coffee.

"Thanks," he said gratefully.

"I put a jigger of your favorite in it," she said. It was a luxury he allowed himself on weekends, a jigger of Irish whiskey in his coffee. It was early yet for the whiskey, but he figured Grendel with her usual foresight knew he could use it.

"She's nice, isn't she, Grendel?" He sipped the coffee slowly.

"And sad. She's carrying a heartache inside."

He nodded. "She can't have had an easy life."

"No, but you can see she's gone on and made the best of it. I like her."

Grendel's praise was hard won, and David knew that Laura had impressed her. Even more than Barbara had when Grendel first met her. *She has some growing up to do,* Grendel had observed, and it was true. Barbara had come from a wealthy family who indulged her in everything — art lessons, music lessons, her own horses, and vacations in Europe. It was a contrast to his own background, and Barbara had intrigued him. She was beautiful and artistic and he was willing to indulge the child in her. They had done well, he thought now. And they'd had a good marriage.

Laura was different from Barbara and yet he felt himself drawn to her as strongly as he had been to Barbara. Her quiet strength filled some void in him. He roused himself as he heard Grendel leaving the room.

"Mary's getting ready for the party," she said. "I rue the day someone invented earrings."

He laughed and watched Grendel's retreating back, thinking how much more slowly she moved now. She needed household help, but she was too stubborn to let him hire anyone other than a cleaning lady twice a week. She had a lot in common with Laura, he thought ruefully.

Frowning, he went to his desk and opened the top left drawer, idly rummaging through old newspaper clippings he'd kept. He didn't save everything — he'd written too many pieces over the years for that — just the ones that intrigued him. And he knew that if he'd read about Laura

Kincaid in the paper he would have kept the clipping. He sat down in the swivel chair in front of the desk and thumbed through the pile. He dug into the drawer again and came up with a handful of old editorials he'd written. When he was full of fire and idealism, he thought wryly. He was beginning to skim through them when he heard "Dad!" in grievous tones from the door.

He saw Mary standing there with both hands on her hips, and he shoved the clippings back in the drawer and went to greet her, smiling. "Ready for the party, sugar?"

"I'm too old to be called that," she protested, ducking the hand that would have rumpled her hair. "And I moussed my hair, so don't mess it up."

"Okay, no sugar and no mussing the mousse." He smiled down at her. "Now what's the problem?"

"Grendel says I can't wear this skirt," Mary wailed.

David sighed and leaned back to inspect his daughter's outfit. The skirt was denim, skin-tight, and it ended a good seven inches above her knees. "Well," he said, trying to sound diplomatic, "isn't it a little brief for January?"

"But *all* the kids will be wearing short skirts."

"The boys too?"

"Dad."

"All right," he said, trying not to smile. "How about a compromise? A skirt, but something not quite so short."

Mary sighed elaborately and shrugged. "I *suppose* I could find something else."

"I seem to remember that after that big shopping expedition last week, clothes were spilling out your doorway and down the hall. My charge card is still smoking."

"Oh, Dad." But her complaint was good-natured and she gave him a smile. "And I guess it's not so bad to be called *sugar* once in a while," she added over her shoulder as she trotted toward the stairs.

David smiled after her and headed for the kitchen, the pile of newspaper clippings forgotten.

"Well, here we are," Laura announced to Horton the next afternoon as she slowed the car in front of David Evers's house. The gate was open and she drove through, feeling like an interloper. When she opened the door Horton bounded out, nearly knocking her down in the process, then snorting into the dead grass in pleasure. "No simple thank you for your chauffeur?" Laura sighed, smiling nonetheless as Horton cantered across the yard toward a squirrel frozen at the foot of a tree. The squirrel bolted up the tree and Horton leaped excitedly. Laura could see his muzzle move as he barked, but the wind carried away any trace of the sound. She started when she felt a hand on her arm.

It was David, and he'd come to greet her in such a hurry that he hadn't put on a coat. And from his grin he was obviously pleased to see her.

"You'll freeze," she warned him, her throat tightening at the sight of his dark hair catching the light as the wind ruffled it, and the sparkle in his oh-so-blue eyes.

"Then come inside with me," he said, taking her hand and pulling her with him.

She had to halt him long enough to get her camera and lenses, and then he was tugging her toward the house again, like an enthusiastic boy. "Slow down," she said, laughing. "I can't run in these shoes."

He turned to face her, trotting backward while he continued to pull her hand. "Grendel fixed some tea and cookies."

"All you think about is food," she teased him.

He grinned and his eyes twinkled devilishly before he answered, "Not all."

Laura was glad the blustery wind gave her an excuse for her reddened cheeks or she would have been embarrassed as Grendel eyed the two of them with satisfaction when they entered. She beamed, poured hot tea, pushed the plate of cookies in front of them on the kitchen table where they sat, and then — she left.

"Where's Grendel going?" Laura demanded as the door shut behind David's grandmother.

He just grinned at her.

"Well?" she demanded, finding his grin infectious and trying hard not to give in to it.

"She's giving us privacy," he said, his eyebrow arching. He popped a cookie into his mouth.

"Grendel likes you."

"I'm here to work," she reminded him, trying hard not to look too long into his face. But he had such a gorgeous, compelling face that she couldn't seem not to look.

He was silent a minute, his eyes studying her, and Laura broke away her gaze and reached for a cookie to still her restless hands. When she looked back at him the grin had been replaced by a gentle, probing look. "Is that the only reason you're here?" he asked.

"I'm . . . I . . . don't know," she said awkwardly. She wasn't used to people dealing with her emotions as directly as David did. He wasn't afraid to ask the hard questions.

"I'm not asking for anything, Laura, not now anyway." His hand moved to her arm, stroking, and this gesture he always used to get her attention now became a caress. Laura felt a pounding in her head, a heady warmth, and suddenly an emptiness because she ached for a man's touch — this man's touch. "You seem so sad sometimes," he said, and she had to strain to read his lips. "What is it, Laura? What makes you unhappy? What hurt you?"

She wanted to tell him about Buddy, about her own insecurities and how Buddy had fueled them until she depended on him for everything. And how Buddy had hurt her. But how could a man like David — an honorable, caring man — understand someone like Buddy Fielding and how he could even make a woman betray her own sense of values? Laura had suspected that something was wrong with Buddy's handling of the school, but he had convinced her that she knew nothing about the matter and that she and the school would be lost without him. And so she had done nothing to stop him until it was too late and he had drained the life blood from the school.

David watched the play of emotions across Laura's face — pain, sadness, a tinge of distrust. Years of living with her deafness had apparently taught her to speak with her face as well as her voice. And yet, in the end, it was quiet retreat that settled over her features, and he knew she would have no answers for him. *Laura, Laura,* he thought helplessly. *Why won't you let me reach you?*

"I guess I'd better get to the office," he said at last, standing. "I've got a meeting. Maybe I'll see you later."

She read the hopeful expression on his face and ached with wanting him to stay and just talk to her. "Maybe later then," she said and watched as he got his coat.

He gave her a lingering smile, full of the kind of tender devilment that made Laura's heart turn over, and then he was gone. She was at war with herself, she thought. She wanted David, physically and emotionally. He was so different from Buddy, and he made her feel more of a woman, more valuable, where Buddy had diminished her. But Laura's indomitable will, that part of her that had carried her through a life adjusting to a disadvantage, through a bad marriage and then scandal, that part said *no. No, I won't hurt like that again. I've come this far, and I won't risk losing it all.*

Rubbing her eyes wearily, she picked up her cameras and headed for the hall. As was her habit, she planned to lose her old memories in hard work.

Chapter 4

The kitchen door banged open, and Horton came barging in, knocking over the light Laura had set up on the floor to add dimension to her photograph of the alcove. Horton was followed a split second later by a shouted, "Grendel! I'm here!"

Laura stood up quickly and found herself facing a freckle-faced woman of about twenty-five whose familiar blue eyes widened in astonishment. "Ohmigosh!" the woman cried. "I'm sorry. I didn't knock you down or anything, did I?"

Laura smiled, recognizing the eyes as David's. "No, Horton just took out the light. But it looks like it'll survive." She held out her hand. "Hello. I'm Laura Kincaid. I'm —"

The girl broke into a grin. "Laura!" she interrupted. "Of course. I'm David's sister Erin. You're photographing the house, right?"

"Yes, that's right," Laura said, taken aback that David seemed to have informed his whole family about her.

"Well, it's awfully nice to meet you. David's shown the first signs of life since he met you."

"You're not bothering Laura while she's working, are you?" Grendel demanded as she

74

strode into the kitchen. "She's busy, you know."

"I know that, Grendel," Erin said, her grin broadening as she picked up two of the cookies from the plate Laura had left on the table because it gave the picture a nice lived-in look. "I just wanted to see if it was still okay to have my meeting here tonight." She handed Horton one cookie and popped the other into her mouth, taming her grin long enough to chew.

"Your meeting," Grendel said, frowning. "I'd forgotten."

"If you have to get things ready, I could quit for today," Laura hastened to say. "I've already been shooting for a couple of hours."

"No, no, dear," Grendel said, waving away her suggestion. "You're not in the way. It's just that I haven't baked anything for Erin to serve tonight."

Erin made a rude noise and gave her grandmother a mock glower. "These women don't want little tea cakes, Grendel. Some cookies will do fine. If you don't have enough, I'll bring some."

"Cheap store-bought cookies that have been sitting on a shelf since the Depression, no doubt," Grendel groused. "No, I'll bake something. Those poor women need something special."

Erin shook her head. "All right. Have it your own way." Laura had been looking from one woman to the other, trying to catch all of the conversation, and now Erin patted her affectionately on the shoulder. "Can you take a break now, Laura? I could use a cup of tea myself, and we can leave Grendel to her baking."

When the tea was brewed, Erin snatched up the plate of cookies and led Laura and Horton to the mammoth living room, where she settled them in front of the fireplace, raising her own legs to rest her boots on the overstuffed hassock.

She said something into her cup of tea, and Laura leaned forward. "I'm sorry, I didn't hear."

"Oh, gosh, I didn't mean to mumble," Erin said, looking at her contritely. "David said you wear a hearing aid."

Laura decided it was best to be forthright, since that's what Erin seemed to be. "I have to do a lot of lipreading, too."

"In that case, I'd better not eat and talk at the same time, which is my usual modus operandi." She gave Laura a sly look. "Something David was always telling me not to do."

"David sounds like he was quite the taskmaster," Laura said, scratching Horton's head.

Erin shook her head. "Not really. I just like to tease him. Actually, David's good humor kept the whole family going when Mom and Dad seemed to be falling apart. He hasn't been as lighthearted since Barbara died." She chewed a piece of cookie thoughtfully, then gave Laura a meaningful glance. "Until you, that is."

Laura gave a wry lift of her brows. "I'm afraid I haven't done much other than cause him trouble with my hearing aid batteries and my dog."

Erin dismissed that with a toss of her dark curls. "That's not trouble for David."

"He was the kind always bringing home strays?" Laura guessed.

"Dogs, cats, other kids, sometimes strangers." Erin's booming laugh filled the room. "God, that used to drive Grendel crazy!" She removed her boots from the hassock long enough to lean forward and peruse the cookies again. "I guess it's genetic. At least that's what Grendel claims when I get going on one of my projects. Hey! I have a great idea!" She turned to face Laura enthusiastically. "Why don't you come to my meeting tonight? It would help to have a few pictures of how we got started and everything. I mean, would you mind? I don't want to impose. And there's a woman coming I'd like you to meet."

Laura didn't know what to say. "I don't know what kind of meeting it is," she said hesitantly.

Erin slapped her palm against her forehead. "God! Forgive my manners. We're starting a shelter house for abused women. A couple of the backers will be here tonight as well as three or four of the women I counsel." She rolled her eyes toward the ceiling. "God, I didn't even tell you. I'm a counselor with the mental health center."

Laura's head was whirling. It was difficult to follow Erin's rapid-fire delivery, especially since she tended to forget to face Laura when she was talking. And she wasn't sure she wanted to get involved with the kind of project that would bring up painful memories from the past. Laura knew enough about battered women to know that she herself had gone through many of the same emotions — that sense of helplessness and the loss of self-esteem. If she came to Erin's meeting, she would have to face those emotions all over again.

Erin placed her hand on Laura's shoulder, a gesture that brought Laura out of her reverie and reminded her of David. "Hey, listen, I don't want to pressure you," Erin assured her. "But David said you were so good with the girls that I thought you might be a good influence tonight."

Laura couldn't help responding to Erin's warmth, and she briefly wondered if she was David's project in the way that these women were Erin's. No, she wasn't being fair to him, she told herself. "All right," she said, smiling at Erin. "I think I'd enjoy getting out tonight."

"Great! Why don't you stay for dinner then, too?" Not giving Laura a chance to answer, Erin jumped up and started for the kitchen. Laura couldn't hear what she said, but she gathered it had something to do with Grendel and dinner.

She looked down and saw Horton watching her, and his eyes blinked. "Well, how could I refuse?" she said reasonably. Horton lay back down with a satisfied smacking of his mouth, and Laura could have sworn he smirked.

David was late for dinner, and Laura felt a

lurch of her pulse when he sauntered into the kitchen and saw her clearing the table along with Grendel and Erin, who was chattering a mile a minute. Laura couldn't miss the pleasure on his face or the way his eyes glowed as they traveled over her hair and face and on down to . . . Well, at least he tore his eyes away when Grendel said something to him about dinner.

"I grabbed a sandwich at the office," he said, still looking at Laura.

"Well, at least you got here in time for my meeting," Erin complained, giving Laura an open grin as she scooped a serving dish from the table. "Although I guess you might have made it sooner if you'd known we had company for dinner."

"Yeah," David agreed amiably. "Might have."

From the corner of her eye, Laura could see Erin observing the two of them from the side of the table, her arms folded over her chest. Finally Erin shook her head and snatched — the way she seemed to pick up everything — a legal pad from the counter. "Here!" she said, shoving it at David. "Go get the living room ready before they get here. And stop staring at her like that or you're going to wear her skin off with your eyes!" She grinned at Laura again and went back to her hasty clearing of the table.

When Laura looked at Grendel she saw that even she was grinning happily. "Oh, this has been a fine week," she said by way of explanation, and then broke into an off-tune hum.

Laura and Grendel were seated in the living room, Laura curled quietly on a cushion at the far corner of a huge sofa, when David and Erin began answering the door, returning each time with a new person. Laura knew that she would immediately be able to tell the potential backers of the shelter from the women who would use it, and she was right. It wasn't just the clothes, because two of the battered women were well dressed, and the other three could have passed for college students. No, it was an attitude. The women who kept their eyes down and hardly smiled — those Laura knew were Erin's special clients. One of them looked around the room helplessly, as though she might sit in the wrong place by accident, and then she caught Laura's eye. Laura smiled, and the woman visibly relaxed and came to sit next to her.

Her name was Patty, and although she was a stocky woman with short, thick hair, it was obvious to Laura that she was frail in spirit. Laura began to talk to her quietly, looking her in the face the way she did with the kids at the Hastings Institute, and Patty soon responded, answering in short, soft sentences. Once Laura had to apologetically ask her to face her when she spoke, and she explained about her hearing.

"Oh, I'm sorry," Patty said, and Laura watched her blink rapidly with emotion. "My little girl has a problem too. The doctor said it's the bones in her ear. He says he can fix it with an operation. I don't know . . . It scares me to think of her in the hospital."

Laura touched the woman's hand. "It's a common operation. And it works. There's nothing to be afraid of."

"But . . . you can't have the operation?"

Laura shook her head. "My problem is the nerve, not the bones."

Erin was tapping a table for attention, and Laura watched her lips as she began delineating her plans for the shelter. Laura couldn't follow everyone who spoke after Erin since they remained seated and often faced away from Laura, but she gathered that support was strong and money was not going to be a problem. She let her eyes rove around the room and found David in a back corner, his eyes on her. He smiled, and she felt warm and secure, as if he'd reached out and touched her hand. When she turned around she could still feel him looking at her, and she thought of how open he and his family were, nothing like the family she'd had growing up. Although Laura's mother had pushed her to be all she could, Emily Kincaid had given up on herself, and the two of them remained shut in their house like a pair of mice hiding from winter.

Erin was asking if anyone had ideas as to what facilities the house should contain, and one of her clients hesitantly suggested a playroom for children; another said a big kitchen. Then Patty stood up and Laura fixed her eyes on the young woman's face to catch what she was saying.

"Rooms with locks and shades," she said firmly. "A room where a woman can go to be alone and know no one's going to come pull her out of there. A room where she's not hiding but where she can be herself." She sat down abruptly, her face flushed from her effort, and Erin broke into a broad smile. "Privacy," Erin echoed. "Write that down, David."

Laura reached over and squeezed Patty's hand. It was just what she'd wanted after the financial scandal at the Fielding School for the Deaf hit the newspapers and then Buddy left her. *A room where a woman can go to be alone.* Laura felt a pang of worry as she realized that she couldn't keep that part of herself from David and his family indefinitely. She was going to have to tell them soon. And then what? The woman permanently associated in people's minds with the Fielding School for the Deaf was not the ideal companion for a candidate for public office.

Erin's other clients had gathered around Patty as the meeting broke up, and Laura felt satisfaction as Patty was enveloped in the tight-knit, caring group. She didn't hear David come up to her, but she sensed his approach and turned to find him just behind her. His eyes, a soft blue in the subdued lighting of the ceiling fixtures, were fixed on her with a riveting intensity. She was conscious of the thudding of her heart in her throat and a dull ache somewhere deep inside, some secret corner of her heart that she'd locked and resolutely turned her back on years ago.

"You look tired," he said.

"I am a little," she admitted, pride refusing to let her tell him that she was exhausted; that the effort required to determine who was speaking when she couldn't distinguish any clear sounds, that the straining to read lips halfway across a room, had all wearied her to the bone. And she had missed more that usual tonight. A woman behind her had stood up to speak, and Laura hadn't realized anyone was saying anything until she saw everyone look in that direction. Only a couple of weeks until her appointment with the otologist, she reminded herself. She had to get this hearing aid checked.

"Laura!"

She saw Erin's mouth form her name as she appeared beside David, but didn't hear it.

"You were wonderful!"

Laura looked at David uncertainly.

"I can't thank you enough for talking to Patty. I don't know what you said, but you worked wonders." Erin beamed. "I just knew you were someone she'd open up to. She was the most withdrawn woman in my group, and tonight was a real breakthrough. I can't thank you enough."

"I didn't really do anything," Laura protested weakly.

"Nonsense. You have a natural knack with people." Erin squeezed her arm and then frowned over at a group of men gathered at the wet bar. "I'll talk to you later. I have to do a little fund-raising over there."

Laura sagged against the arm of the sofa when Erin left and David took her by the arm. "Come on," he said, turning so she could see his face. She could read the worry in his eyes, and she wondered what was wrong. He led her out of the living room and to the small alcove where they'd eaten dinner. Horton, lying in the corner, jumped up and wagged his tail.

"You're going home," he said, opening the closet and taking out the white wool coat she'd worn there and his own leather jacket.

"I'm all right," she responded testily. "And you're tired yourself."

It was true. The lines at his eyes had deepened during the evening, and his mouth was tight. She knew he was pushing himself for this campaign, and she didn't want him fussing over her when he was ready to drop himself.

"No arguments," he said, trying to soften the words with a ghost of a smile as he held out her coat for her.

She shoved her arms into it, then pulled herself away from him, fastening the buttons with a frown, her eyes on her hands and not him. His imperious manner reminded her somehow of Buddy, though Buddy was always pushing her to do more when she was exhausted, not less. *You can't be that tired*, he would complain. *At least show up at the party with me. And for heaven's sake, don't wear that ugly hearing aid.* And she would go and sit at the party, nearly falling asleep, not able to understand any of the conversation around her without her hearing aid, and miserably watch Buddy charm some group of moneyed widows.

She didn't fit in then and she didn't fit in now with David and the family and friends surrounding him. She couldn't kid herself. It would always be an exhausting fight to communicate in the hearing world, something David took for granted.

She turned when David touched her arm. He was frowning down at her, and he'd put on his own jacket, turning up the collar.

"Are you going to tell me what's wrong?" he demanded, not letting her look away.

"Nothing's wrong," she said shortly. "I'm going home. Come on, Horton." Glancing at him before she turned away, she added, "And I don't need an escort."

He caught her arm and turned her back to him. "I'll walk you to your car," he said sharply. "I'm leaving for a meeting anyway."

"I can manage," she said quickly, pulling away from him and hurrying out into the night. The January wind nipped at her bare throat and teased her coat around her legs. Laura shivered and reached for her car door.

She froze when his hands touched her shoulders, and he turned her around to face him. "Laura, what's wrong? What is it?"

She stared at him, at his handsome face with those probing blue eyes, now a stormy gray-blue, at his dark hair ruffled by the cold wind, and she ached with longing for him. She knew she should stop this before she got any more involved with him and his family. She should go back to her own silent world and let him live his life with the hearing. She should go before . . . before he kissed her and she was lost. His hands framed both sides of her face, and their warmth was a sharp contrast to the icy wind. Despite the storm in his eyes and the traces of anger around his mouth, she knew he was going to kiss her, and she wanted him to. She wanted him to kiss her more than she could say.

She couldn't hear what he said, but she saw his lips move. "Don't fight me, Laura. I'm not the enemy."

Yes, he was.

His mouth touched hers ever so slowly, and the tension drained from her body. She leaned, unresisting, yielding, against him. David gathered her in his embrace, his mouth pressing for more, summoning a response from deep inside her. . . . She tasted him hungrily. She kissed him back with the clamoring emotions of a woman who had *wanted* this for so long, but had denied it with her heart because it could never be hers. She had lied to herself, had convinced herself that there was no flame within her ready to burn at a man's touch, because she had thought there would never be a man who would touch her like that. And now she was ready to cry for what she had denied herself and for what she would have to relinquish eventually. She could never have this man because they came from two different worlds.

Her breath caught on a stifled sob, and she pulled away from him. "I have to go," she managed to say. "I can't . . . Good night, David."

She turned away so she wouldn't see his answer and fumbled with the door. He opened it for her and Horton jumped in first, clambering over to the passenger's side. She slid in then and stared straight ahead as David closed the door. When she could control her fingers, she dug her keys from her pocket and started the car. She dared one glance at him before she pulled away, and her heart knocked against her ribs in pain. He was standing like a statue, his hands jammed in his pockets, and on his face was the same need and desire that were pounding inside her.

She drove until she was a mile from his house and then she had to pull the car to the curb and give vent to her frustration. She pounded the steering wheel and let out a piercing wail that came back to her lifeless ears as a thin, reedy vibration. She didn't fall silent until Horton leaned over and lovingly licked her face.

Chapter 5

"Use a basting stitch," Laura directed Mary, who was hunched over the sewing machine, frowning in concentration. Laura had been photographing the immense living room from different angles when Mary had arrived home from school, trailing a swath of material and wailing that her life was ruined because she was going to fail home ec and *nobody* but an idiot failed home ec.

The source of her grief turned out to be a skirt, and Mary had botched several attempts to make an elasticized waistband. Laura had sewn many of her own clothes when she was growing up, mainly because there was little money for off-the-rack items. She had calmed Mary down and set about helping her right the offending waistband.

Laura had arrived at David's house late both yesterday and today, not wanting to see him after the way they had parted the night of Erin's meeting. But he had been gone both times, and Laura had invented excuses to turn down Grendel's dinner invitations.

Now she helped Mary pull the threads to gather the waistband and then insert the elastic. "Well, I'm no expert," Laura said as Mary held up the finished skirt, "but it doesn't look like an idiot made it to me."

Mary grinned sheepishly. "It looks like something from *Little House on the Prairie*, but it ought to get me a passing grade. Gosh, I'll be glad to get out of that class. Who wants to learn how to make biscuits anyway? All I need is directions to the dairy case in the store."

Laura couldn't help laughing. Mary's irreverence was becoming more endearing the longer she knew the girl. Mary still treated her a bit warily, as if she didn't quite know how to act, and Laura knew it was natural for the girl to feel a little resentful of her. After all, she was the interloper who was taking their father's time.

"My turn," Jean announced, pulling Laura toward the desk. They were all in Mary's room, and Jean had brought in her own schoolwork. The younger girl was more open and had formed an attachment to Laura, an attachment that made Laura feel guilty even as she enjoyed it.

"And what's your project?" Laura asked.

"I have to do a map of Mexico." She held up a box of colored pencils.

"Spare me!" Mary exclaimed. "Those stupid pencils are for nerds."

Laura had grown adept at reading the girls' lips, and except when one of them turned away from her, she rarely missed any of their conversation.

"Are not!" Jean protested. "Are they, Laura?"

"No, of course not," Laura soothed her.

"Now let's see your map." She smiled at the neat, painstaking outline. "What's this?" she asked, pointing to a star.

"That's Mexico City. I have to draw in the rivers too."

"Well, honey, we'll have to move Mexico City a bit. The last time I was there it was a smidge farther north."

"You were in Mexico City?" Jean asked, her eyes wide.

"A long time ago," Laura said, feeling the pang of old memories. She tried to put the image of Buddy seeking donations from the wealthy Americans living there out of her mind, along with the pain of remembering. She had stood at his side and accepted the check along with him, a sense of pride filling her. But it was short-lived pride. Only a week later, the financial discrepancies were uncovered, and Buddy and Lori Fielding found themselves on the front page of the newspaper. The Mexican check was eventually returned.

Laura realized Jean had said something and looked up from the map.

"What did you do there?" Jean repeated.

Laura's throat constricted. How could she ever make a child understand what had happened in the past? "Nothing, honey," she said quickly. "It was just a trip. Come on. Let's finish your map."

Laura didn't hear the sound, but both Jean and Mary turned toward the door, and Jean cried, "Daddy!"

Laura slowly turned toward the door, her pulse thready and weak. She felt the familiar race of her heart as she anticipated teasing blue eyes and an engaging smile.

But the David watching her now was hesitant. He was leaning against the doorjamb, his suit coat slung over his shoulder, but his eyes belied the casualness of his stance. She could see the worry there and the unspoken questions. He didn't know how she would receive him after their last parting.

"I thought maybe everyone would like to go get some ice cream," he said, but his eyes never left Laura.

She swallowed and tried to summon a smile as Jean hugged her father in her excitement and Mary studied her nails nonchalantly. "I guess so," Mary said, "if I can get that White Lightning sundae this time."

"How about you, Laura?" David asked, and in his voice she heard him also asking if things were okay between them.

"I could go for a Turtle Supreme," she said slowly. "Sewing skirts and making maps works up an appetite."

David relaxed then, and his smile was genuine. "Come on then," he called. "Let's get going before Grendel gets home and makes us eat a proper dinner."

He took them to the shop where he'd first taken Laura, and this time they had a different waitress. While Mary and Jean ran to the counter to ogle the varieties of ice cream, David leaned back wearily in his chair and watched Laura. "You have a knack with the girls," he said. "You're all they talk about anymore."

Laura gave a small shrug. "You've done a wonderful job with them — you and Grendel."

She didn't realize her eyes had strayed to the window until he touched her hand and jolted her back to the table. He was studying her face with an intensity that made her acutely aware of how attractive he was. She stared back at him, thinking that she needed to talk to him, but unwilling to break the spell his blue eyes cast.

"Laura," he said gently, his thumb moving restlessly and hypnotically over the back of her hand. "I mean it. It wasn't an idle compliment. Sometimes you look as though you don't believe compliments, as if they'll be followed by some rebuke."

His directness caught her off-balance again, and she struggled to regain her equilibrium in the face of his tenderness and the sensual assault on her hand. "I'm not very good at receiving them," she said simply.

Why not? he wondered. She should have received a lot of them. She was such an open, vulnerable woman, and yet she had the kind of tensile strength that he suspected could endure much more than she'd told him. And when she looked at him like this he could see some distant sadness in her eyes, something she hadn't told him about. He wanted her to talk to him and to trust him, but for some reason she wouldn't.

She turned slightly and the light caught the small aid in her ear. At the same time that reserve in her face almost made him remember something — or someone.

"Laura," he said, the pressure of his fingers bringing her attention back to him again. "I'm not sure how to ask this, but have you ever been written up in an article? Sometimes you look so familiar —"

He broke off at the sudden change in her face. Her eyes had turned to crystal and her cheeks drained of color. The soft hand he had been stroking stiffened beneath his touch. *She looks like a wounded animal,* he thought, and had no idea why.

"David —" she began, and she seemed to be making a supreme effort to deal with something. Then he saw fatigue wash over her, and she closed her eyes briefly. "No," she said quietly. "No, it's not important."

"Laura, you can talk to me," he said in frustration, watching as her eyes slid away, effectively shutting out all communication. He released her hand and sat back, composing his face as the girls returned, bubbling with enthusiasm for their favorite ice cream treats. He stole one more covert look at Laura and found her absorbed in what the girls were saying. Only the high spot of color on each cheek betrayed her emotions.

Before he turned his full attention to his daughters David made a vow to himself. *If I have to move heaven and earth, you're going to talk to me, Laura.*

Laura caught sporadic glimpses of David the next several days as his campaign efforts appeared on the local news and in the newspapers. Each time she saw his picture it caught her unawares and sent a sharp pain through her. She was deceiving him, she told herself as he was interviewed on the news, and yet she felt her pulse race at the mere sight of him. His eyes looked tired and strained, and Laura longed to go to him and erase that strain. But she brought herself up short with the reminder that what she had to tell him would do nothing to ease the pressure. He was running a campaign and still putting in a full day at the newspaper. She knew he came home exhausted and late almost every night, and what little time he had left he spent on his daughters. No, she wasn't going to make him deal with another burden. She longed to talk to him about Buddy and the Fielding School, but it wouldn't be fair to him. And if someone found out — it could throw a pall over his campaign.

She had almost finished the pictures of his house the day he had taken her and the girls for ice cream, and now she deliberately stayed away from his house, staying late at the office and getting caught up on her other assignments. "Go home," Beth told her early Friday afternoon. "You look exhausted." Laura nodded gratefully, and Beth said, "Is everything all right, Laura? I

94

know it's none of my business, but — well, did something happen at David Evers's house?"

Something had happened, all right. Laura had discovered that inside herself there lurked a warm, loving woman starved for a man's touch — a particular man's touch.

"No," she said, trying to smile for Beth. "Routine."

"Um-hmmm, sure," Beth observed, crossing her arms and giving Laura one of her don't-try-to-con-me-kiddo looks.

"It's a long story," Laura said apologetically. "And I don't think it's going to have a happy ending."

"Laura, I'm sorry," Beth said immediately, touching Laura's hand in sympathy. "Anything I can do?"

"No, but thanks for asking," Laura said. "Hey, maybe there is something you can do," she said when she was almost to the door. She grinned at Beth. "Buy me a drink this weekend."

"You're on," Beth said, grinning back.

It was still early, so Laura took the bus to the Hastings Institute. She poked her head into Anne's office and, seeing she was on the phone, gave her a wave and a smile. Anne signaled Laura to come in, so she took a chair in front of Anne's desk. Watching the woman's animated face as she talked, Laura couldn't help thinking how fortunate it was that she had met Anne and that Anne had befriended her.

After Buddy and Laura were ousted, Anne,

the wife of a well-to-do lawyer, was brought in to run the board of directors while the school was reorganized. Anne was also the mother of a son with a severe hearing impairment, and she had more patience and strength than Laura had encountered in anyone before. Anne heard stories of the work Laura had done from the teachers at the school and had come to see her. "I'm not doing this out of pity or any desire to embarrass you," Anne had said in her no-nonsense way, "but they tell me you're damn good with these kids and I want you to stay on."

It was Anne who suggested that Laura use her maiden name after the divorce and drop the nickname Buddy had given her, Lori. And it was Anne, along with Beth, who encouraged her when she was feeling down and who listened when the frustration with college and not being able to catch everything the teachers said overwhelmed her. Because of them, Laura had kept going, gotten her degree, and then taken the job with Beth.

"You don't know how glad I am to see you," Anne said when she hung up the phone. She sat back in her chair with a weary smile.

"Bad day?"

"The worst. More red tape with the government. One teacher quit because her husband got transferred to another state. Two kids got into a fight on the playground, and one got a nosebleed. And Clara came back for the first time today."

"How did it go with Clara?" Laura asked anxiously. Clara was one of her favorites, and the three-year-old girl was having problems adjusting and learning.

"Not good," Anne said, shaking her head. "She couldn't wear her aid for two months after that last bout with ear infections, and now she's forgotten how to listen. And her father and mother separated recently, so her mother has a lot to deal with and not as much time to work with Clara at home. She threw a tantrum during fingerpaint time with the other kids in her class today, and poor Julie finally had to put her in a room by herself." Anne threw out her arms in a gesture of surrender and said, "You won't reconsider, will you, and become assistant director? I'm still serious about the offer."

Laura shook her head. "It's tempting, but . . . well, you know how I feel about any bad publicity that might hurt the school."

"I think you're wrong about that, Laura." Anne's sharp eyes were serious. "The furor died down a long time ago, and anyone who knows you realizes you had nothing to do with what Buddy did."

"Thanks for having confidence in me," Laura said, smiling as she stood up. "I think I'll go check on Clara."

When she glanced back at the door Anne was watching her pensively.

Laura found Clara in a small, bright room with posters of *Sesame Street* characters on the walls. She was sitting in a corner, methodically slamming a plastic pail on the floor. Laura recognized the pail as one the children used outside in the sandbox, but this one was bent from Clara's rough handling.

Julie Hart, one of the assistants, looked up from her seat near the door as Laura walked in and gave her a relieved smile. "Boy, am I glad to see you," she said.

"It sounds like she put you through the wringer today."

"You've got it. She wore herself out and fell asleep for a while, but when she woke up I offered to give her some milk and cookies if she'd say 'cookie' for me and we got off on another tantrum. Listen, could you watch her for a while for me? I could use a cup of coffee."

"Sure. Go ahead." Laura leaned against the doorframe and watched the little girl give vent to a fury that wouldn't abate, and her heart went out to her. Laura had gone through the same thing trying to learn to listen with the hearing aid and experiencing more frustration that she'd ever known in her young life. Even now, she occasionally found rage welling up inside her when some simple task confounded her because of her lack of hearing. It still exhausted her to try to keep up with a group conversation, and it was the memory of these frustrations that made her sympathize with Clara.

"What's the matter, Clara?" she said soothingly as she walked across the room toward the girl. She stopped to beat her fists on the table, and that got Clara to finally stop and glance over her shoulder. Seeing Laura, Clara gave a flicker of recognition and then went back to her tantrum.

Laura knelt beside the girl and picked up the toy chick from the table where it lay among a pile of toys and books. She suppressed a sigh as she let her eyes travel over Clara's dark brown curls and the furious stiffness of her shoulders. *It's so hard, isn't it, baby?* she thought. Then she hid all traces of despair and gently but firmly turned Clara around to face her. "Look at the chick, Clara," she said loudly and clearly. "How does the chick go? Peep, peep, peep."

Clara's stormy blue eyes briefly turned up to Laura and then she pounded the floor again, her piercing wail perceived as a faint whine by Laura.

"I know, honey, I know," Laura said, instinctively reaching for the girl and cradling her to her. Clara fought her a moment, her body rigid, her muscles still trembling with rage; and then her body relaxed slightly against Laura, and Laura stroked her hair and cheek. Still on her knees, Laura held and rocked the child until most of the anger was gone and the wails had subsided to grunts. Then she picked up Clara's favorite picture book from the table and carried Clara to the rocking chair in the corner where she sat down.

She pretended to read the book herself for a

while, covertly watching as Clara cast furtive glances at the book and finally abandoned herself to her curiosity, staring at it as Laura turned the pages. "Look at that bus," Laura said to no one in particular. *"Bu bu bu. And there's a cow by the side of the road. A cow goes moo moo."* Laura exaggerated the sounds and made appropriately silly facial expressions, and soon Clara was glancing from the book to Laura's face. Laura began to make up a story, since the book was a child's dictionary, and soon she'd incorporated a dog going *bow wow* and a cat *meow*ing. She further embellished the story, confidentially adding to Clara that the bow wow couldn't hear anything because he wouldn't wear his hearing aid and so he didn't know how to *bow wow* right and it came out *ow ow*. Clara was entranced, although Laura guessed that she still wasn't comprehending much of what was being said. Still, it was a start when Clara hesitantly pointed to the picture of the dog again, and Laura said "Bow wow!" loudly, repeating it over and over.

Then Clara grunted and began to climb off her lap, and Laura knew that the lesson was over. The children's patience often ran short with the lessons, and it was best to let them end it themselves until they could understand the concept of a time limit. On top of that, Clara had lost the discipline she'd recently won, and Laura knew she couldn't be pushed now.

Laura stood up with a sigh and sensed someone standing in the doorway. "She's lost ground,

Jul—" she began, stopping short when she saw that it wasn't Julie, but David there.

"I didn't mean to interrupt," he said, his eyes searching her face.

"You didn't," she managed to say. "Clara ended the lesson herself." She barely trusted her voice to ask the next question. "How long have you been there?"

"Quite a while," he said vaguely. "Beth told me you were here and I asked Mrs. Tyler where I could find you."

Laura felt a surge of heat, part desire kindled by the sexy look of him leaning against the door, and part anxiety that any second he would put together the names "Hastings Institute" and "Lori Fielding."

"I thought maybe you'd like to have dinner with me," he said after they'd stared at each other in silence. He didn't look at all sure that she'd accept.

"That sounds good," she said. "I'll just get my coat and find Julie. Excuse me a minute."

She brushed past him breathlessly, anxious to speed their departure. She caught a whiff of his clean, soapy scent and felt her knees weaken, but she pushed on down the hall.

Laura found Julie in the coffee room and made a quick report on Clara's progress. David was coming down the hall as Laura and Julie walked back toward the room, and as Julie went on ahead Laura saw her give David a keen, interested appraisal.

"Ready?" David asked her as he helped her on with her coat.

She nodded and began walking briskly toward the front door.

"What's the hurry?" David asked as he caught up with her. "You're not that hungry, are you?"

She tried to mirror his teasing smile but gave a shrug instead. "Tired, I guess," she said, stepping into the brisk wind and pulling up her coat collar.

"Rough day?"

"I suppose so. Clara was doing so well before."

He helped her into his car and got in the other side, turning sideways to face her before he started the engine. "Why's she having problems now?"

"Oh, a lot of reasons." Laura frowned. "She had several ear infections, so she couldn't wear her aid. And then her parents split up, so her mother couldn't spend the time at home working with her." She let her voice trail off and stared out the window. "I don't want to bore you with this."

His fingers touched her chin and turned her back toward him. "You're not boring me. I asked because I want to know." There was a slight edge to his voice, a tiredness that Laura recognized; and something else as well. He was waiting for her to say something, but she didn't know what it was.

Apparently he stopped waiting, because he

withdrew his hand, started the car, and drove off.

Laura was expecting him to take her to a restaurant in the city, and she was surprised when he turned the car onto the highway. They drove without speaking for a long time, and finally Laura felt she had to break the tension between them. "How's your campaign going?" she asked.

"All right. Tiring, I suppose. I don't get the time with the girls that I'd like . . . or with you."

He cast her a sidelong, appraising glance, and she flushed. She wanted to reach out and put her hand on his arm, to touch the coiled strength she had felt before in his embrace, to stroke the large hands and gentle face; but she held her want carefully in check.

"I don't want you to take time away from your campaign for me," she said defensively, trying to put up just one more roadblock and yet making the mistake of looking into his face. This would be so much easier for her if only that determined, lonely look wasn't in his blue eyes. She realized she was trying to tell him things couldn't work between them, but the words just weren't coming out.

"Laura," he said, putting his hand over hers and taking his eyes from the road a moment to give her a piercing look. "I don't want to pressure you, but I guess I figure at my age there's no point in being coy. I haven't made a secret of the fact that I want you. So I'm going to ask you straight out — is it yes or no?"

She waited, trying to frame a coherent answer to his question, but only burgeoning desire forced itself into her head, not answers. And she couldn't tell him no when she couldn't seem to stop looking into his face or move her hand from his warm caress. She felt helpless to stop something she never should have started.

He was giving her a choice, and she couldn't deny herself any longer. Let the past go to hell. She badly needed a slice of heaven in the present.

"It's yes," she said, her throat tight from the pounding of her heart.

He turned to look at her, giving her a slow, heart-stopping smile. "Yeah?" he said.

"Yeah," she said, smiling back shakily.

"Hot damn," he whispered.

He turned down a rural road, the crunching of the tires on the gravel imparted to her more through the vibrations of the car than through her hearing aid. Through the window she watched the wind buffet the stark, bare trees and push powdery gray clouds across the sky. They passed a couple of farmhouses, and then he was turning onto a frozen dirt road, which rocked and bumped the car over the rust and stones. At the end, almost hidden by a stand of cedar trees, was a small log cabin. Beyond it lay a pond.

"Welcome to Evers Swamp," he said, the tightness of his hands on the steering wheel belying his easy smile. "Barbara gave it its name. She didn't particularly enjoy coming here, although she was a good sport about it."

"It's not so bad," Laura said, looking around and seeing that, despite the run-down condition of the cabin, the place was beautiful in its solitude. She felt drawn to it instantly.

"Come on," David said as he opened her door and pulled her out. He fumbled with a lock on the door, then shoved it open and let her walk in first. She was relieved that it was clean. She could live without rugs and wallpaper, but had there been a mouse or snake waiting to greet her she would have turned tail and run.

All in all, the cabin was very nice, she decided as she looked around while David built a fire in the fireplace. It was one big room: a kitchen in the corner, divided from the rest of the room by a breakfast bar; a living room, with a couch and two chairs arranged in front of the fireplace; and what she supposed was the bedroom in the opposite corner, a small single bed with an old quilt thrown on top. The place looked as though it had been cleaned recently, and Laura looked questioningly at David when he stood up from the fire.

"Do you come here often?"

"Not anymore," he said, and there was regret on his face. "I came by yesterday and sort of put things in order. Aired it out and put some food in the refrigerator. I needed to get away this weekend after all the hassles of the campaign."

To get away alone? she wondered. Apparently not, she noted as he took two steaks from the refrigerator. He heated a skillet on the stove and dropped on the steaks while she sat at the breakfast bar to watch him. He seemed preoccupied, and Laura took the opportunity to study him. He had apparently gone home from work to change before looking for her, because he wore jeans and a dark blue wool sweater.

She could see why he was popular with the press and the public. His physical attractiveness was magnetic. There was a strength in his face, in the sculpted cheekbones and unyielding jaw, and especially in the blue eyes with their dark lashes and brows. But there was compassion there as well, a tenderness that came out at unexpected moments. She had seen it often with his daughters and with herself. He would win the primary, she decided.

His movements at the stove had stilled, and now he turned to face her. "What are you thinking about?" he asked, the hint of a smile teasing his mouth.

"About the election," she said honestly, and his smile grew.

"Alone in a tiny cabin with me and you're thinking about an election," he said, laughing. Then he grew serious. "Does the election bother you?"

She wasn't sure what he meant, and shrugged lightly. "I figure you'll win easily."

"Why?" Seeing her expression change, he said, "No, really. Why?"

Laura took a deep breath. "Because you're

you, that's why. I can't imagine why anyone wouldn't vote for you." He was giving her a wry smile, and she added, "And you have good ideas. I've been reading about you in the newspapers, and it's obvious you've thought things out for a long time."

He leaned against the stove and crossed his arms. "Oh, have I? Thought things out, I mean."

She realized that the conversation had shifted, and he was talking about something else now, about him and her. "Yes," she said slowly. "I think you have."

They both looked at each other a long time, and then he casually reached around, turned off the stove, and then looked at her again. "Come here," he said softly, turning toward her, his mouth an enticing invitation.

Laura stood, her heart pounding, her blood singing some song long forgotten, and walked slowly toward him. He took two steps and then enfolded her in his arms, crushing her against him. The strength of his embrace nearly bruised her ribs, but she didn't care. This was what she had wanted from the day she first saw him, and now she knew it. For the first time in her life she felt no void inside, only a consuming hunger that obliterated everything else.

Her pink silk dress tightened across her breasts as she leaned back to look into his face. His eyes glazed with heated desire as his hands moved upward, his thumbs finding her already engorged nipples and stroking them through the clinging fabric until they hardened into peaks. He lowered his head and gently brushed each one with his mouth. Laura moaned with the force of her need.

His mouth sought hers and captured it, kissing her with the strength of a man who had hungered for this for a long time. His hands came up to cradle her head as he marauded her mouth with increasing pressure. At last he raised his head a fraction and stared down into her eyes. Laura couldn't hide the longing she knew was mirrored there. "David," she whispered brokenly, and he kissed her again, this time softly, his mouth barely brushing her tender lips.

"The bed's not much," he said by means of wry apology.

"I don't care," she assured him. "It's you that matters, not the bed."

His thumbs slowly caressed her jaw, his fingers framing the column of her neck. Like the trembling of a tree in the wind, a slight shudder ran through him as he stared at her through thick-lidded, passion-filled eyes. "It's not just because . . . of what you mean to the girls or the brightness Grendel says you've brought back to the house," he explained carefully and with shallow breath. "It's because of what you mean to *me*, Laura. You know that, don't you?"

No, she didn't know it, and even now it didn't seem important. He might think differently later, she reminded herself. But even that warning wasn't enough to cool her passion or consuming need for him. They needed each other now, and that was enough for the moment.

"Yes," she said softly into his sweater, not knowing if he heard or not.

"Come here with me." He led her to the bed and sat down, pulling her onto his lap. "Is everything all right . . . with us?" he asked quietly.

"I don't know," Laura said, her hands moving restlessly to stroke his chest through the sweater. "Is it?"

"Talk to me, Laura," he told her, his breath coming in short rasps as she moved her hands beneath the sweater and felt the velvety smoothness of his midsection and the mat of springy hair above. "If there's anything wrong, I want to know. Tell me, honey."

Tell him about Buddy. She wavered, her eyes seeking his, wishing for understanding. Her mouth opened, but the very vulnerability in his face stopped her. Telling him now would only hurt and devastate what was happening between them. She couldn't barter away this moment for a clean conscience. Desire was too long buried, and she knew she would grieve forever for this lost afternoon if she lit it slip through her fingers. She wanted David, if only to build sweet memories, and he was hers right now.

"It's nothing," she said, lowering her eyes so he wouldn't see the lie in them, and then she lifted his sweater and brought her mouth to his clean, hard chest. His swift intake of breath told her he was thinking only of the sensations she

109

was creating, and she touched each flat nipple with her tongue, running her fingers softly down his ribs.

David pulled his sweater over his head and tossed it onto the nearby chair. He tilted her back until her head rested on his shoulder and then he began slowly undoing the front buttons on her dress. Laura couldn't hear their breathing, but she felt her own whispery intake and the matching rhythm in the rise and fall of his chest. His fingers weren't steady, but neither were hers when she tried to help him.

That made them both laugh shakily, and he kissed her again. His mouth began a thorough exploration of hers, his teeth catching her lower lip and holding it still for his tongue to tease and tantalize. Laura felt a sound rise in her throat and she held it back, letting only a sigh escape.

David leaned back slightly so he could see her eyes. "Relax," he told her gently. "I won't hurt you."

"I . . . know," she said. *But I'm scared.*

He seemed to know that, too, and spent a long time caressing her arms and face as he slowly undid her dress. When it was open he slipped his hand inside and softly squeezed her breasts beneath her bra. She twisted on his lap, wanting more, burying her fingers in his thick hair and pulling his mouth even closer.

He lifted her and let her dress slide down, and Laura kicked off her high heels, stockings, and half-slip. He stood up, removing his own shoes, socks, and jeans. Instinctively he seemed to know how to minimize her feelings of vulnerability, to make himself as unclothed as she was, physically and emotionally.

She bit her lip when he eased one finger under the waistband of her panties, and he stopped, gave her an off-center smile, and brought her hand to his waist. "You first," he said, standing still with that same smile while she tugged down his underwear. He was as gorgeous naked as her fantasies of him, and she couldn't stop her eyes from traveling over his lean male angles, sinewy and muscle-honed and taut. He was so tall and graceful and darkly handsome that it made her blood pound a sensuous rhythm just at the sight of him.

His gaze held her eyes while he slid down her panties, his hands gliding over her hips and thighs, blazing a trail of fire. He followed the trail back upward with his mouth, leaving her shaking with passion when he kissed her stomach. "David," she groaned, hardly able to bear much more of this sweet assault.

"I want you so much," he said, standing up and restlessly stroking her shoulders. "But I'm trying to make us both wait so it will be good."

"Let's not wait," she teased him, letting her fingers trail down his chest and then lower. She watched with pleasure as his cheeks flushed in desire.

"Wait, hell," he groaned. "You'll be lucky if I wait until we're in the bed." He reached out to cup her face and Laura froze, her laughter dying. Her head flooded with Buddy's words — *How much pleasure is it if you can't hear a damn thing I say?* Unconsciously, her hand had covered David's, stopping him as his hand moved toward her ear.

He looked into her face and she saw no condemnation there, only mute puzzlement. "I . . . I can't hear anything at all without it," she managed to get out.

"Would you rather keep it on?" he asked, his finger retreated gently, carressing her cheek.

Laura stared into his eyes and what she saw there gave her the courage to shake her head. "No," she said firmly. "No." She removed the aid, and then her bra, and she laid them on the chair with the rest of their clothes. She found herself shivering, more from anticipation than from the slight chill of the cabin, as his eyes, stark blue and filled with fire of their own, roved over her body. But what truly trembled was her heart. She felt as though she'd been freed from some prison as she stood there in her profound silence, unable to detect the crackle of the fire, and read his face. The silence didn't matter. Her world this minute was David and only David.

He eased her onto the bed and brushed the hair back from her face, and then his hands and mouth roved over her at will as he lay beside her. Laura felt his mouth on her thigh and a vibration on her skin there as he murmured something.

David. She couldn't hear herself, but she felt

112

the word whisper from her throat. In an instant he was looking down into her eyes again and she said, *David. Let me see your face when you talk. Please.*

He smiled again and brushed his finger down her cheek. *All right, honey,* he said. *How's this?* His hand moved down the length of her body, making her blood collect in every secret place, as he smiled down at her, and Laura put her arms around him to pull him to her. *Now,* she murmured. *I need you now.*

He levered himself on top of her, and, poised and waiting, he looked down at her. Laura's eyes meshed with his, and they spoke a language that needed no sound. At the moment he entered her, she felt such a rush of pleasure that she cried out. She turned her head to the side in despair, because Buddy had once told her the sounds she made during lovemaking were like some animal's, but gentle fingers brought her face back to his. And there was no distaste on his face or criticism, only a fiery passion that beckoned her.

She found that they needed no words and sometimes she wasn't sure if she'd read his lips or just his face. He was an artful and strong lover, and he brought her the kind of pleasure that was total abandonment. *I need you, love,* he beckoned, and she matched his rhythm. *Yes, love. Oh, yes.*

You're mine. David's mouth formed the words — or was it just the light in his eyes? Laura wasn't sure. Memory slipped beguilingly away from her as his body moved with hers, giving her such sweet pleasure that she felt her breath escape in rasps.

Thought spiraled away into pure sensation, and Laura felt her nerves dancing at the edge of a precipice. *David, David . . .*

I'm here, love. I'm here with you; you're so soft and sweet.

It feels so good, David.

I know, honey. And with a deep, burning passion in his eyes, his hands clasping Laura's face in pleasure, David carried them both over the precipice.

David, I think I might love you. As Laura slowly swam back to wakefulness after a drowsy interval in David's arms, those words floated into her head. She couldn't remember if she'd said them out loud or not. Sometimes when she wasn't wearing her hearing aid she didn't know if she spoke or not, and on the twilight edge of sleep now she couldn't remember.

She looked at the man lying next to her, one leg thrown over her thighs in male possession, his fingers idly stroking her arm. His eyes were half-shuttered, his dark hair tousled, his beautiful body damp with perspiration.

I'm never leaving this bed again, his lips said, and he gave her a lazy, proud grin.

Laura stretched under the weight of his legs and shivered slightly. *You're cold,* he said immediately, and pulled the blanket up over both of them. She shook her head, smiling, but he tucked her in more tightly anyway. *I ought to insulate this place better. Barbara always said it was too* — He broke off and gave an apologetic twist of his lips, but Laura's heart had jerked the moment she saw Barbara's name on his lips. She lowered her eyes so he wouldn't see her sudden dismay, and they lay there together several more minutes, neither moving.

He touched her cheek finally and she looked at him. *Are you hungry?* he asked, summoning up a cheery smile for her. Laura nodded, and he rolled out of the bed, patting her hip before he went. *This was pretty nice,* he assured her with a devilish raise of his brows.

It had been more than pretty nice, she thought, but now she was back to reality and she had to face two things — the ghostly presence of Barbara, and the fact that David still didn't know about Lori Fielding. *David,* she said quietly and he turned around from the chair where he was pulling on his pants. But she couldn't seem to tell him. Not with the glow of their lovemaking still on her body. *It was darn nice,* she agreed. He grinned and hopped on one foot as he tugged on a shoe.

Chapter 6

It was dark when they finished dinner. Laura felt mellow from the wine, and she had eaten her fill of steak, salad, and baked potato.

She had rinsed her plate and was leaning against the sink contentedly, ready to volunteer to do the dishes, when David slipped his arm around her shoulders. "You ready?" he asked, grinning.

"Ready for what?" She was suspicious of the twinkle in his eyes.

"For the ice skating, of course," he said innocently. "Didn't I mention that?"

"No, you know very well you didn't mention that!" she accused him, and he laughed.

"Must have slipped my mind," he said with so much earnestness that she almost believed him.

"Oh, sure, David." She was beginning to catch his playful mood. She still hadn't decided if he was teasing her or not.

"You don't have to hurry home to let Horton answer nature's call or anything, do you?" he asked, and she thought she saw worry on his face at the prospect she might have to leave.

She shook her head. "I have a neighbor who walks him when I'm not home."

"Then you couldn't possibly have any objections to ice skating, could you?" he said, grinning again.

"One, it's freezing outside. Two, I don't know how to ice skate. Three, I'm wearing a dress —" she began, enumerating all the reasons why he wasn't going to get her anywhere near a sheet of ice just waiting to dump her on her rear end.

"The only time to ice skate is when it's freezing outside," he informed her, "and I think Mary has some old warmup suits around here that would fit you. You're taller, but I'm sure I can rustle up a pair of long socks to keep you warm where the pants end."

"You're serious about this, aren't you?" she said, seeing that she was being railroaded.

"Mmm-hmmm." He was clearly enjoying watching her try to wriggle out of this, and he stood leaning against the sink with his arms crossed, trying to tame an escaping grin.

Laura gave an exaggerated sigh for his benefit. "Well, I suppose if you're intent on bringing me up here just to kill me, then I don't have much choice."

"You're such a good sport, Laura." He laughed, tugging her toward him and giving her a hard kiss. "Come on. Let's get you some suitable clothes."

He insisted on watching her change clothes, making cute little comments about the fit of Mary's warmup suit and enjoying the sight of her in various states of undress entirely too much. Laura told him so.

"Oh, I know," he assured her. "This is more fun than I've had in — well, since we got in bed." He grinned again.

He made her sit down while he had her try on some old skates from a chest in the corner. "Don't I get training wheels?" she complained. "I had training wheels on my bicycle."

"No, you don't get training wheels," he told her. "I'm going to be beside you the whole time. Now let's go."

The wind had died down, and the crescent moon had risen high over the black silhouette of the trees. The ice on the pond reflected a silvery glow and Laura could feel frost crunch beneath her feet. They sat on an old log beside the pond, and David helped her lace up her skates. Then he led her out onto the ice. She went awkwardly, feeling clumsy bundled up in the assortment of cast-off clothing he'd made her put on, with the biggest offender of all being the darn skates. David had given her an old red jacket with a hood and a drawstring at the bottom. The jacket was enormous, and, though she had tightened the drawstring around her hips, she couldn't do much more than flap her arms helplessly within the magnitude of it.

"Now let me see your form, Kincaid," he said, letting go of her hand.

Laura squealed. "Form! My ankles are dragging the ice here, David, and you're talking form!"

"All right, all right," he soothed her, looking as though he was trying very hard not to laugh. "We won't talk form." The laugh escaped anyway. "Darned if you don't look like a big candy apple!" he told her.

"You're too easily amused," she said as he chortled. "Athletics were never my forte."

"Oh, yeah? And what was your forte?"

"Certainly not ice skating," she informed him.

"Come on. What were you expert at?"

Exasperated, Laura muttered, "Piano tuning!"

"Piano tun—" he began, and then it struck them both as incredibly funny. They laughed so hard that Laura abruptly found herself sitting down on the ice, not at all sure how that had happened.

"Are you okay?" David asked, bending to help her to her feet, his laughter resuming when he saw that she was indeed unhurt.

"Somebody pulled the ice out from under me," Laura complained, and that got them started again. When her laughter eventually faded, she was breathless from it; she was also in David's arms, a very smooth maneuver on his part. But it was nice. Especially the way he was smiling down at her, his blue eyes even more beguiling in the moonlight.

And then she realized that she was skating. Or rather David was skating and pulling her along in his wake. He was gliding effortlessly backward and Laura was following, not entirely under her own steam. She let herself relax and quietly drift

119

in his arms, feeling the air cool her heated face. This was a different silence than the one she felt without her aid. This was a silence of consent, a silver silence, she decided. Without her aid, silence usually felt leaden.

Laura's skates wobbled, but she gradually managed to keep her ankles from dragging the ice and soon she lost herself in the sensation of floating in David's arms. The air bore the sharpness of a cracked icicle and the moonlight gave the illusion of being as frozen as the last tangles of foxtail beneath a layer of hoarfrost. The night was endless. She could remember, as a child, standing in the middle of the old iron bridge with its wooden flooring, alone in the summer twilight, listening for cars and scampering across to the other side when she heard one coming. She was five then and she could still hear. After the meningitis and after she fell into the world of silence — when she was well enough to walk again but not yet fitted with her hearing aid — then she used to go back to the bridge; it seemed as though she had left her childhood on it long ago. Only then she had been afraid to step onto the boards or to grasp hold of the iron framework or take even one small step toward the middle. It was as though her world had shrunk and that bridge went somewhere she could no longer go.

One winter day her mother walked with her to the bridge and must have seen the fear in Laura's eyes. She touched her on the shoulder and motioned for her to go ahead and walk onto the planking. "I can't, Mom," Laura had protested, shaking her head. "I can't hear the cars come anymore. What if I was in the middle and one came?"

"It's wide enough, honey," her mother had said, bending down and motioning so Laura could understand what she was saying. "Trust the bridge."

Laura had stood rooted to the spot for what seemed like an eternity, and her mother had pretended to be busy watching a crow in a nearby tree. Finally Laura had taken a tentative step onto the first wooden plank and then another. When she was in the middle, she'd stopped and just stood there, her heart pounding in excitement and triumph. She'd looked back and waved to her mother and then gone to the side and stood there, holding the railing and looking down into the trickle of a stream, its top thinly crusted with ice.

A car had come eventually and still Laura had stood there, feeling the planks vibrate beneath her feet as the car crossed the bridge and remembering how it used to sound like thunder. The driver, an older man, had waved to her, and she'd waved back. When she'd left the bridge, she was grinning.

Trust the bridge. It had come to mean many things in her life. When something was difficult she would repeat the phrase to herself and remember her mother. And she had learned to trust other bridges in her life, those tenuous spans between life's experiences. Trust in them and you went from one place to another. You grew and you learned.

And so she thought of the bridge as she skated across the silvery ice, and she knew she had come a long way from the days of Lori Fielding to be skating in David's arms. She had crossed a lot of bridges and she wasn't the same woman.

Imperceptibly they slowed, and when she glanced quizzically at David he was watching her through shadowy blue eyes, his head slightly cocked. "Laura," his mouth said, and she knew he was whispering. "I think I'm falling in love with you."

"I think I'm falling in love with you too, David." She was whispering too, as though the night and the moon were listening to everything they said. "I need to talk to you," she said, but her words were lost against his mouth as he pulled her to him. He was so warm, buffering her from the cold, his mouth moving over hers softly and then pressing hard. Her hood had slid off, and he smiled as he raised his head. His fingers caught her hair on both sides of her face and brushed it back. Reflexively Laura turned her head slightly away from him, hiding the hearing aid that was now visible, it was an unconscious gesture she'd picked up from the days of Buddy's complaints about her "ugly ear piece."

"What is it?" he asked, hands still in her hair turning her face back to him.

"Nothing," she assured him, quickly pulling a piece of hair over her ear again anyway.

"Laura," he said, "I don't know what the hell hurts you or has hurt you in the past, and you won't tell me. All I know is I can't stand that look you get in your eyes sometimes."

"I don't know what look that is," she said stubbornly.

"That look like somebody just pinched you and you don't want to cry and you don't want to tell on them either."

She just stared at him helplessly. This was one thing about David she still wasn't quite accustomed to — his way of just coming out and saying something and demanding to know what was the matter. Buddy had — No! She had to stop thinking about Buddy. He was in the past, and he had no place in her thoughts with David.

"Don't you see?" David said, his hands tight on her arms. "I want to know you — to know everything about you, Laura. I don't care what it is. I said I'm falling in love with you and I'm damned if I'll let you shut me out. Maybe you can't hear very well, but I'll follow you as far into that silent world of yours as you'll let me."

Remembering the iron bridge made her plunge in. "I was married once, David," she said, so quietly that she didn't hear her own voice, just felt it humming in her head, saying words that might change how David felt about her. "He — my husband — hated my hearing aid. He said it was ugly. But he hated it when I took it off too, because then I couldn't hear anything. It was a no-win situation," she said dryly. *Tell him the rest,* her head cried, but her pride kept her silent.

The pressure on her arms eased. "I'm sorry, Laura. So sorry."

"Don't feel sorry for me, David. Please."

"Hell no," he said with feeling. "I feel sorry for the bastard who didn't know what he had when he had you." He started to say something else and then frowned down at her. "Are you cold?"

She hadn't realized she was shivering until he asked, and then she saw that her fingers holding his collar were trembling. The cold air and the force of her emotions had exhausted her. "A little."

Apparently he was going to respect her reluctance to talk about her ex-husband because he helped her back to the log and began unlacing her skates. "Oooooh," she said, leaning back as he pulled off one skate.

He smiled. "Are your feet sore?"

Laura nodded. "My ankles. Dragging the ice didn't agree with them."

David unlaced the other skate. "Barbara used to complain of the same thing. The skates are permanently scuffed."

Laura's breath caught and held as she realized she had been wearing Barbara's skates. Again, she felt like the interloper. This was Barbara's husband, and those were her children and her cabin and pond. Laura had no right to them.

Lori Fielding had even less right.

David wasn't looking at her as he sat down to unlace his own skates, and Laura ducked her head as she tugged on her shoes. She felt a dark misery spreading inside her like shadows on the icy pond. She had felt this so often since she lost most of her hearing — this feeling that she didn't belong. She hadn't belonged in grade school with the other children who could hear each other call out instructions on the playground when they played Red Light. She hadn't belonged in a marriage where her husband found her hearing aid ugly. She hadn't belonged in the Hastings Institute because her ex-husband had nearly closed the place down with his greed. And now she didn't belong with David. Only she *did*. She wanted to belong so much.

He touched her arm, and she wouldn't look at him until his fingers brought her chin up. His eyes were probing her face. "You're not crying, are you?" he asked gently. "What is it, Laura? Is it your — ex-husband?" He said it sadly.

"It's the cold," she said to explain the tears gathering in her eyes.

"Let's get you inside." He pulled her to her feet, chafing her hands in his, his eyes still fixed worriedly on her. Laura tried to give him a reassuring smile.

Inside the cabin, he fixed her a brandy while she sat on the hearth, warming her hands in front of the blazing fire. She was lost in her own thoughts, and when she looked up she saw that

125

he had set the snifter in front of her and was studying her profile.

"It's not the cold, is it?" he said when she looked at him.

Laura stared down at the floor and then met his eyes again. "No," she admitted.

She saw his chest move as he sighed tightly. "Laura, I don't want to play guessing games with you. I care too much for you to do that. Whatever happens between us, we have to work on it together."

She saw that he was making an effort not to touch her, to force her to work through this with him, and she knew he was right. And yet, she wasn't ready to talk about her past. She was falling in love with David, and for her own selfish reasons she wanted to keep what she had with David separate from her past — as far from memories of Buddy as she could get.

"David," she said gently, reaching a tentative hand to touch his hard jaw and then letting her fingers slide to his sweater. "You're bound to make . . . certain comparisons between me and your . . . wife." She had picked her words carefully, giving him part of the truth, but not all of it. She didn't tell him that she had already made those comparisons and they had been painful for her.

"Oh, Laura." He said it again and then grasped her hand, holding it to his mouth to kiss her palm. "I'm sorry. I didn't mean for this to happen."

"You don't have to be sorry," she said quietly, anxiously scanning his face. She didn't understand what he meant.

"What an idiot I've been," he said, shaking his head ruefully. He gave a short laugh. "Well, of course you'd do that — compare yourself to Barbara and wonder if I was doing the same — since I took every opportunity to remind you."

"I'm sorry?" she said in her turn, not understanding.

He gestured around the cabin. "This place, my car, the skates. I've kept Barbara's things around so long that I forget how it must seem to someone else." He looked into Laura's eyes, and she felt her heart stop. "I'm sorry, Laura."

He was still holding her hand, and she tightened her fingers on his. "It's all right," she told him. "It's only normal. You and Barbara were a family for a long time."

He was silent, studying her face and frowning. "You're talking as though you don't have feelings, as though it doesn't matter that I did something that hurt you," he said slowly. "Why? What happened, Laura? Did your husband make you feel guilty for simple, human emotions?"

"I never had the kind of marriage you had with Barbara," she said hesitantly, feeling her way through an emotional minefield. She hadn't thought about her marriage for so long, hadn't wanted to deal with it, that her memories felt rusty. "Barbara was kind and loving and artistic.

Bud— my husband was a cold, insecure man who never learned how to give, who could never make life give him enough to make up for his childhood. He made me feel cold and insecure in turn. He didn't know how to nurture. He only knew anger and dissatisfaction." Suddenly she realized that her face was wet, that she was crying and the tears were running down her cheeks. "Oh, hell!" she muttered as she suffered the final insult to her dignity, having David see her cry. "And I don't want your sympathy, David."

"Dear God, but you're one tough woman," he said with a mock groan, finally eliciting a faint smile through her tears. "All right," he said. "No sympathy. But if you'd do me the favor of resting your head against me here like this" — he tugged her stiff form until she was indeed lying against him — "then I think we'd both start feeling a whole lot better. There. No, now don't go moving on me. I really need this." She coughed and wept against him, and he held her head and stroked her hair.

She couldn't hear everything he said, but she felt the rumble in his chest and it made her feel better. When her crying had stopped he gently turned her face up to his. "Sometimes it's tough going," he said softly, "whether the marriage is good or bad. And sometimes it's tough going when you meet someone new and you try to let go of the past. You have to work at getting to know this new person in your life. You have to understand what they've been through. I want to do that, Laura. But sometimes I don't know what to ask you or what to say." He ran a knuckle down her nose. "So if I don't do the right things sometimes, or say the right things, I'm still trying, Laura. I'm trying my damnedest. I'm just not used to this."

"You do great," she told him with feeling. "Damn, David. I'm not so used to this either."

He laughed and pressed her tightly against him. He rocked her a minute more and then he held her away and looked into her face. Rubbing the back of her hand over her eyes, Laura tried to look into the fire instead of at him, but she couldn't do it. His eyes were too compelling, not to mention his crooked smile and the way he cocked his head to the side as he watched her. "Look at me," he told her. "I'm going to tell you something, and I want you to understand everything I say."

"David —"

"Now don't say anything. Just listen."

"But David —"

"Shhhhh. You can ask questions when I'm done. Now listen." He lowered his head to peer into her eyes to make sure she was listening. "I had a good marriage. You had a lousy one. We agree on that much. Now, does that make us incompatible?"

"Not in theory," she said.

"You're worried about Barbara because I was happy with her. And I guess I'm not as worried about your husband, because you weren't happy with him." He stopped and looked at her hard. "All right. Maybe I'm a little worried. But not a lot. Now be quiet just a minute longer — and quit poking me with your finger just because you want to interrupt! I'm going to tell you something about Barbara." He took a deep breath and slowly pronounced. "You're not her."

"Oh, now there's front page news," Laura said dryly.

"Hold on, and let me finish. I'm not looking for any substitute for her or someone just like her or anything like that. I feel what I feel for you because you're you, Laura, and not because I'm comparing you to Barbara and you've added up to the right number of points or something." He frowned a minute and rubbed his chin thoughtfully. "What I shouldn't have done, though, is have all these reminders of Barbara around. Not much tact on my part." He looked at Laura again and gave her an apologetic grin. "I get to keep the kids, but anything else you don't want around can go."

Laura shook her head and put her arms around his neck. "I don't want to throw things out of your life," she said softly. *I just want to come into your life.*

They sat that way a long while on the hearth. Laura with her head resting on his chest, her arms around his neck. She felt the heat of the fire and the steady beat of David's heart.

"You know what?" he said at last, tilting her

130

head up so she would see his mouth form the words.

"What?"

"I'm going to show you what a principled man I am."

"Oh, yeah?" she said, mildly interested.

"I want you so bad I can hardly stand it, but I'm going to deliver you back home to Horton right now so you can get some rest." He stood up and pulled her up by her hand.

"You're a regular Royal Mountie, aren't you?" she said, slipping her hand beneath his sweater to stroke his warm, firm chest.

"Don't tempt the Mountie," he warned her in a husky growl.

"Of course not," she said indignantly, still stroking. Her lips were beginning to curl into a teasing smile.

"Of course not," he repeated softly, his hands moving to her shoulders and massaging restlessly.

"David?"

"What, Laura?"

"I don't want to go home and rest."

"Mmm-hmmm," he said in distraction, his mouth brushing her nose and then her cheeks and finally closing her eyes with feather kisses.

Laura glanced at David as he drove, and she yearned to massage away the tension in his shoulders. The campaign was hard on him, especially when it took him away from the girls.

After Buddy, Laura had harbored cynicism for anyone in the public eye, whether they were entertainers or politicians. But in David she had discovered the best reasons for serving the public — a genuine desire to improve things.

David had dropped by her apartment the night before, tired and hungry, and she had fixed him a sandwich and some coffee. It was already February, two weeks since they had made love in the cabin, and David's schedule had precluded any real intimacy between then since then. He'd said he wanted to be with her this weekend, but he had a meeting . . . So here she was, going to a political dinner on a Saturday night.

And she knew the reason he was tense. He hadn't come out and said it, but she knew he wasn't sure how she would accept this political life of his. He had stayed late at her apartment the night before, leaning forward on the couch to run his hands through his hair, talking earnestly about the need for better roads in the state and the possibilities for revenue. She had found herself caught up in his excitement, and for the first time she looked beyond David the lover, the father, the newspaper editor, and she saw all the good he could do.

Laura touched his arm and smiled when he looked at her. "Your speech will go fine," she assured him. "Your ideas are wonderful."

He relaxed then and answered her smile. Laura felt a moment of panic when he turned the car into the huge parking lot of the lodge where the dinner was being held and it struck her that there would be an enormous crowd in attendance; but she kept smiling for David's sake.

"David! You're here!"

David had just opened the door when the short, beefy man with receding hairline and a brow puckered in perpetual worry clapped him on the shoulder. "Come on!" the man urged. "They're serving the fruit cups already!"

"Artie, Artie —" David began, trying to pry the man's attention from the sheaf of notes he was consulting as he trotted them down the hall toward the meeting room. "For God's sake, Artie, wait a minute!"

"What!" Artie demanded, coming to such a sudden halt that Laura nearly bumped her nose on his chin as he spun around.

"I want you to meet Laura," David explained patiently. "Laura, this is Artie Hempstead, my campaign manager. Artie, Laura Kincaid. And don't read while you talk to her. She wears a hearing aid and needs to see your lips. Okay?"

"Yeah!" Artie said, pumping Laura's hand, popping an antacid tablet into his mouth and shuffling through his notes, all with one hand and seemingly at once. "Now come on! Fruit cups are on the table!"

David grinned at Laura as Artie surged ahead to greet a few people still milling around the meeting room entrance. "Well, what do you think?" he asked.

"I think he talks in exclamation points," she observed.

David laughed. "He has his whole life. In first grade, our teacher told Artie he was going to be one of two things — an opera singer or a drill sergeant. She used to have Artie lead the whole assembly in the Pledge of Allegiance."

"Come on!" Artie called as he poked his head out of the crowd. David gave Laura a raise of the brows as he propelled her before him.

The way to the head table was long and winding as David stopped to say a personal word here and there, introducing Laura and reaching across heads as someone new would stand to shake hands. David had an excellent memory for names, and he seemed relaxed and perfectly natural as he greeted one supporter after another. Laura kept her eyes on his face, switching to the face of the person in front of David as soon as David introduced her.

It took all of her concentration not to miss any important words as she focused on each person's mouth, so she didn't have the luxury of looking on down the row of tables.

It was therefore with total shock that she looked into the next face and recognized Ralph Harvey, one of the investors in the Fielding School for the Deaf — the man, in fact, who had instituted the investigation that culminated in Buddy's and her ouster.

Laura couldn't say anything for a moment, and gradually she realized that he hadn't recog-

134

nized her. He was smiling and shaking her hand and saying how nice it was to meet her.

"Very nice to meet you,' Laura murmured, hoping David would quickly move to the next person. When she glanced at David she saw that he was watching her worriedly.

"Are you all right?" he asked quietly, and she nodded.

David moved on, reluctantly it seemed, and when Laura dared a glance over her shoulder at Harvey she saw that he was staring at her curiously. She couldn't seem to breathe or to look away, and then the woman at Harvey's side said something to him and he turned his attention away from Laura.

Nervously Laura raised a hand to her hair and realized that the gold comb securing her hair to one side had come loose and that the hearing aid was visible. Maybe that was why Ralph Harvey was staring, she told herself, but still she couldn't slow the frantic beating of her heart. She followed David, smiling and nodding, acknowledging introductions until they reached the head table, and then she took her seat beside him.

She talked with Artie on her right during the meal and with the woman and her husband at the end, both area organizers of the campaign. Each time she felt David's eyes on her, Laura glanced at him. She would find him studying her covertly and he would smile when he caught her eye. She felt a warm glow inside. As much as she had grown to hate crowds after her public fall with Buddy, this throng of people surrounding her didn't seem to matter, and she realized it was because David was with her. He had become an anchor for the center of her universe without her even realizing it. And with him here she felt she could do almost anything. It was as though she had crossed the iron bridge all over again and now she stood triumphantly on the other side.

When dinner was done the man at the end of the table rose to make the introductions. He gave David's credentials and finished with: "And now, I give you the next state senator from our district, David Evers!" David walked to the microphone to enthusiastic applause and Laura smiled as she watched Artie pop another antacid tablet into his mouth.

David was sincere and direct and his speech was interrupted by applause several times. Scanning the faces in the room, Laura saw rapt attention and approval. It struck her suddenly that David might very well be the next state senator. The reality had not hit her until now. And it also struck her harder than ever that her past could hurt David in the campaign. He could lose a lot of potential voters if someone found out he was seeing the former Lori Fielding. She *had* to talk to him, and soon. Unconsciously her eyes strayed to Ralph Harvey, but his eyes were glued to David.

When David's speech ended he and Laura mingled with the crowd again, shaking hands and accepting praise. Laura stiffened as they approached the table where Ralph Harvey had been, but he had apparently left, and Laura let herself relax a little.

The drive home was cold and she shivered until the car heater warmed up. She deliberately looked out the window, not wanting to face David just yet. She had to find the words somehow. Lord, this was worse than she'd ever imagined. What was she supposed to say? *By the way, have I mentioned that I was once involved in a public scandal?*

She looked over when he pulled the car to the curb under a streetlight a few blocks from the lodge. A few snowflakes were swirling in the dusky light, chased in circles by the wind. David switched on the radio to a soft love song and turned to face her, laying his arm over the back of her seat.

"Can you spend the night at my house, Laura?" There was stark need in his eyes and voice, despite the weary shadows around his mouth. "I know you're tired," he said. "And I appreciate what you did for me tonight."

"I didn't do anything," she demurred.

"Yeah, you did. You spent a long evening with a crowd of people you didn't know, and you wore yourself out trying to keep up with all the conversations . . . and you did a damn good job of it, too. Even Artie — and Artie doesn't take to new people right away — even Artie said you were great." He gave her a lingering smile. "And he said it with an exclamation point."

"Well, that's high praise indeed," she teased him, smiling back. Then she sobered and glanced away briefly. "David, I need to talk to you."

When she looked back at him he seemed so tired and forlorn that she wanted to take him in her arms. He reached out a finger and lightly brushed the back of her neck. "Does that mean you won't come home with me?" he asked, and he sounded sad.

She shook her head. "No, I want to be with you, David."

"Then we'll talk later," he said. "I need you, Laura."

He pulled the car away from the curb and drove toward his house, the soft music on the radio filling the lonely spaces in her heart. She would tell him the truth, she promised herself. In the morning she would tell him about Buddy and Lori Fielding, and about the Fielding School for the Deaf; and then, if he wanted to end their relationship, she would face that too. But not tonight. She wanted one more night of loving him.

As they pulled into the drive the weather report came on the radio, and the forecast was for a heavy snowfall. Already the wind had picked up, and as they got out of the car tiny, hard flakes pelted their faces and hair.

The house was warm, and after he hung up their coats he picked up a note on the kitchen table. "Perfect," he said, giving her a smile.

138

"Grendel is staying in town near the bakery because of the forecast, and the girls are sleeping over at a friend's house."

"We have the house to ourselves," she said softly.

David nodded. "Let's go sit in front of the fire."

They settled in the vast living room in front of a blazing fire that reflected dimly on the panels of ceiling fixtures above, giving the room a warm, inviting glow. Laura leaned back on the beige sofa and kicked off her heels. David reached behind his head for the worn afghan with its frayed threads at the edges, and then he stared at it a moment. "It's time I got rid of this," he said in a husky voice, and before Laura could say anything he picked it up and carried it to a storage closet at the end of the room. He didn't have to say it for her to know Barbara had made the afghan. He didn't have to remove it either, but she felt glad that he did. She didn't want to fight any ghosts of Barbara tonight, not even in her head. She wanted David all to herself just this one time.

"There," he said, coming back to stand in front of the couch. His eyes roved over her hungrily as he loosened his tie and unfastened the cuffs of his white shirt, rolling the sleeves up above his elbows. He looked so handsome, she thought. His charcoal gray slacks were crisp and tailored and emphasized his trim hips and muscular thighs. The white shirt and blue silk tie brought out the gleaming highlights in his dark brown hair and the intensity of his blue eyes. She felt a thrill course through her as she looked up at him, and she realized he had brought out a sexual side of her nature that had existed in limbo all of her adult life. Never before had she felt so appreciated as a woman as when David looked at her like this, his eyes darkening with a fiery passion meant for her alone.

"You are such a beautiful lady," he whispered. She read his lips, savoring each word; there was something special about seeing words on a lover's mouth and not just hearing them. The words became part of David, and she cherished them as though they were an exquisite gift he had placed in her hands.

He lowered himself to the couch with a deep, throaty sigh that made her heart sing an answer to the need she heard in him. She had taken pains to dress well for the dinner tonight, and she saw in David's eyes that her care had been effective. She felt her breasts grow heavy and tighten with desire beneath the ice blue silk dress. This was the first time she'd worn the dress since she had seen it in a store window two months ago and bought it on a whim. It was too dressy for the office with its scoop neck and puffy three-quarter sleeves, but she had fallen in love with it, twirling in front of her mirror at home and loving the feel of the billowing full skirt. The sash was made from the same blue silk, and she had knotted it in the front.

"Come here," David invited, pulling her over until she lay across his lap, her head cradled against his raised knee. "This was all I could think about all through that speech at dinner."

"You're such a pushover, Senator Evers," she teased him. "What if I'm a political action committee of one? Think of all the pet projects I can wangle from you."

"Just name them," he told her, nuzzling her neck and making her tremble with desire.

"Well, there's this study I want to do on the sexual behavior of the congressional male," she said, burying her fingers in his hair and luxuriating in its silky texture.

He chuckled against her neck. "Well, I hope it's *this* congressional male you're planning on studying."

"Mmm-hmmm. Definitely."

"Laura," he said gently, tugging her attention back to what he was saying as he raised his head and studied her. "I'm not a state senator yet, you know. There's a long road before the election: the primary, and, if I win that, then the general election. And tonight's dinner was only a small sample of all the dinners and meetings and crowds in between. Lots of crowds, Laura, and lots of meeting people, some of them none too — diplomatic." She knew what he was telling her — and what he was asking too. He wanted her to know that it would be hard. It would be hard for both of them, but especially for her. But he wanted her with him.

"I know," she said. "But the pay's great, right?" she couldn't resist adding.

He laughed, a rumble from deep inside his chest. "Let's get started on that study of yours," he murmured, and his hands cupped her face as his mouth sought hers hungrily. Laura's lips parted beneath his, and she arched her body against him. A soft, purring sound escaped her mouth as David's tongue slid between her lips and explored the warm recesses, claiming all of her as his own.

"Oh . . . David," she whispered in a feverish pleasure when he raised his head.

"Come to bed with me," he said huskily. "I was planning on a quiet, long evening in front of the fire before we went upstairs, but I can't wait. I want you so much, Laura."

He stood up, pulling her up with him and dragging her against his chest for a long, probing kiss that left her breathless and dizzy. He brushed back her hair and looked into her eyes, and Laura stared back, knowing her own eyes reflected hunger and a need she had never shown another man. David gave a soft groan at the expression on her face, and it dizzied her all over again knowing she had moved him.

She leaned against him, one arm around his waist, as they walked upstairs to his bedroom, stopping every other step to kiss and giggle like love-struck teenagers. Halfway up the stairs he took off his tie and dropped it, and her sash landed on the next step. They were almost to his bedroom door when his shirt had its close encounter with the carpet; her dress fluttered to the floor just inside his bedroom door.

"I can't understand," he murmured, bending to nibble her neck before his fingers slid her slip off her shoulders, "why you can't keep your clothes on."

Laura clucked morosely as the slip hit the floor. "They seem to have a mind of their own." As she spoke she unfastened his belt and tossed it aside. They were in the dark, and David turned on a small lamp on the bedside table. She watched as he took off his pants, and then he stood before her naked, both of them breathing erratically. Eyes locked and held. Pulses skipped. And a voice in Laura's head said, *You love him.* It was true. She loved David the way she had never loved any other man. What she had thought she felt for Buddy was a trifle, a feather in the wind compared to this. For this man she would give everything.

The lamplight glowed golden on his body, and her heart filled with the beauty of him. The hair on his chest arrowed down past lean hips and over his flat belly to the pale skin of his thighs, and she let her eyes glide the same path, loving every muscle, every bone, every inch of male skin.

Without pause, her eyes drowning in his, she removed the aid from her ear and set it beside the lamp. The silence swallowed her, but she didn't notice. A language of the eyes was all she needed. Slowly she discarded her bra and then her panty hose.

She watched his mouth as he told her how beautiful she was, and her heart beat like wings fluttering in a cage. He walked toward her, and Laura felt every restraint melt away. She couldn't hear the low moan she made, but she felt it rise through her chest and throat like a phoenix taking flight. And then she was in David's arms and he was lifting her onto the bed.

It was like being born again, her flesh coming alive under his mouth and hands, her every nerve and pulse point throbbing with the knowledge that this man was hers. His lips caressed her nipples to hardness. As he kissed her between her breasts and on down toward her belly she could feel him murmuring love words against her skin. The words seemed to penetrate to her marrow, as did his kisses, searing her with his need.

His hands stroked her hips and then his mouth was moving even lower, finding the achingly soft place between her thighs. She gasped and reached to stop him, but he caught her hand and kissed the palm, the kiss moving on to her legs and finally to the sweetness that was moist and warm for him.

She watched his eyes as he raised his head to look at her, and she moaned with the passion that filled her to overflowing. Her hands moved unconsciously, forming love words in sign language, and he watched her, his fingers pleasuring her almost beyond endurance. His head bent to kiss her again, and Laura clutched him to her.

He moved to a position beside her, his head propped on his hand as his other hand stroked her breasts and ribs. Laura let her fingers wander of their own will, down his chest and over his belly. When she touched him lower she felt his breath catch, and she looked into his eyes. They were so blue and filled with such stark desire that she forgot everything but this man in bed with her. *I want you,* his eyes said. *I need you so much.*

He tilted her head up, and she saw that his eyes were dark and molten. *Enough,* his mouth said. *I can't wait any longer. I want you now.*

Strong hands pulled her upward until her head rested on the pillow next to his masculine, dark one. *Beautiful lady,* his lips said as he slid over her, his knee parting her legs. His fingers slipped down, dipped into the warm, moist flesh that was so eager for him, and made her arch with her need to have him inside her.

I want you, her hands said in their agitation, her fingers forming the words swiftly and without thought. *Come to me.*

And as he filled her she made small sounds, feeling them in her throat and not caring how she sounded. This man gave her so much pleasure in bed and out and she gave everything she had to him in this moment. *I'm yours, everything I have and am.*

Oh, the pleasure, love. She wasn't sure if she'd

thought it or seen it in his eyes or on his lips. And she felt more loved and cherished in this hour than she had in her lifetime. Her heart spilled open to him, and her fingers moved ceaselessly, caressing his back with urgent messages, speaking the language of lovers.

He caught her hand on the pillow and held it to his mouth, kissing it. *Tell me,* he said as Laura watched his lips. *Tell me what your hands are saying. It's so beautiful.*

She flushed as she looked at her own hand, seeing her middle and ring fingers folded in, the other fingers and her thumb raised. She hadn't really known until now when her heart said it before her head realized it.

I love you.

Show me, he told her. *Help me say it the way you do.*

He copied the position of her fingers and then laid his hand with its love message gently against her lips. He was moving inside her again, and Laura felt the irresistible pull of pleasure's peak. She was drawn higher and higher like a snowflake on the wind, tense and waiting . . .

I love you, their hands said.

His mouth covered hers, his breath mingling with her own. He gathered her to him in one last, possessive embrace and then her body trembled with release and she was drifting, drifting . . .

David lay on his side, propped up on an elbow, the sheet at his chest. He was watching Laura

146

sleep, thinking how beautiful she was, and how giving. He felt as though he had been looking for her for a long time without knowing it, and now that he'd found her he was complete.

He was replete with love, and yet he wanted to take her in his arms and make love to her until they both cried out again. Looking at her sleep, he was sure he could never get enough of her.

Slowly he moved his fingers into the sign she had shown him and he lightly touched her hair with it. The graceful, unconscious way she had spoken with her hands during their lovemaking had taken his breath away, and had made him realize that her lack of hearing was replaced with other senses, other talents and blessings.

She was different from Barbara in so many ways, and yet she was fearless in a way that Barbara had never been. Laura was the kind of woman who took her life and fashioned something beautiful from it, the way Barbara had fashioned art from bits of paper and paint. He could not have run for the state senate when Barbara was his wife. She couldn't have withstood the public pressure. But Laura, even with the burden of her virtual deafness, took it in stride.

He got out of bed and padded to the window to look outside. The snow was falling heavily now. It looked as though they would get several inches. This was the first truly peaceful night he'd had in a long time, locked away with Laura while the snow drifted quietly outside. He glanced back at her and smiled. Her left hand, lying on the sheet, was signing in her sleep. He wondered briefly if she could hear in her dreams or if they were a continuation of her silent waking world.

The soft light from the lamp touched her hair and cheeks, and for a minute she reminded him so strongly of someone that he began to search his memory. A young woman with blond hair that fell past her shoulders . . . No, she wasn't wearing a hearing aid. The memory was so dim . . . She was signing to someone with her and she looked frightened. He closed his eyes and tried to remember. Who was it Laura reminded him of?

A press conference! That was it! He had covered a press conference for the newspaper years ago. A couple was being investigated for fraud in connection with the management of a school for the deaf. *Fielding. Buddy and Lori Fielding.* And they stood on a stage answering the press's questions. Only Lori couldn't hear the questions so someone was signing them to her. David remembered another reporter had asked her something — how did she feel now that the school was going to close? She'd watched the interpreter sign the question and then she'd faced him, her face animated with fire and anger, and he dimly heard the interpreter say the words as she signed. *My feelings aren't important. It's the children who matter. And closing this school will hurt them far more than it will hurt me.* He remembered thinking that *there* was a woman with guts. It was too bad she'd fallen in with someone like Buddy Fielding.

Lori Fielding. Laura was Lori Fielding. He stared at her as the revelation washed over him. She couldn't be, but she was. The truth was staring back at him from his own bed as her fingers moved slowly and dreamily. The same hands, the same animated face, so touching in its strength and innocence.

Everything fell into place now. Her nervousness when he said she looked familiar, her reluctance to have him linger at the Hastings Institute. And last night. He had briefly wondered why she should look so stunned to meet Ralph Harvey, but it made sense now. The man had been a big investor in the Fielding School for the Deaf.

Why hadn't she told him?

He was surprised at the strength of his own hurt that she had kept something like this from him. He was in love with her; he'd told her that in every way he knew how. But she had kept one part of her life hidden from him.

Frowning as he studied her, David pulled on his robe and headed for his den. He realized he was going to have to pour himself a scotch before he reread those old clippings.

Chapter 7

Half-asleep, Laura reached for the man beside her and came awake when she encountered only sheets and a pillow. She sat up and blinked against the bright light from the window. She could see David pulling a sweater from his drawer but the light hid his facial expression from her. For a moment she just looked at him. Tall and lean, he seemed almost predatory in his stance, his chest bare, droplets of water clinging to his dark hair and glistening on his shoulders. His bare toes made furrows in the plush carpet.

"I didn't know you got up," she said, and he turned to face her, his face still hidden in shadows. Laura reached over to the night table and picked up her hearing aid, anchoring the small plastic piece in her ear.

He said something, but she couldn't quite hear him and she still couldn't see his mouth.

She tried to smile lightly. "I'm sorry. I missed that. Can't hear a thing till I've had my first cup of coffee."

She expected a teasing reply, but there was none.

"David? Is something wrong?"

She felt as though she were holding her breath

until he stepped away from the window and gave her a tight smile.

"It looks like we got about six inches of snow last night," he said.

She couldn't hear his voice to judge the tone, but his face looked strained. She started to ask again if everything was all right but stopped herself. She had no right to press him. "I'm a big fan of Old Man Winter," she said. "I used to love to play in the snow."

"Maybe we could take a walk later if you feel like it," he said, pulling the sweater over his head. He sat down on the edge of the bed and began pulling on socks and shoes without looking at her.

"Sure," Laura said uncertainly, trying to see his eyes and not succeeding. She waited, but he didn't say anything else. She slid out of bed and picked up her clothes on her way to the shower. Something had gone wrong. She didn't understand what it was, but she felt a grayness about this morning that all the snow in the North Pole couldn't dispel.

He wasn't in the bedroom when she came back, but a pair of jeans, a white sweater, and socks lay on the bed. Laura looked at them for a few moments, then took off her dress and slip and put on the other clothes. They were a just a little loose, and she guessed that they were Erin's.

He was pouring coffee when she got to the kitchen, and he glanced at her, then back to the counter. "Thanks for the jeans," she said hesitantly.

David nodded and pushed a cup of coffee in front of her. "Erin always keeps some extra clothes around here."

"David," she began helplessly. "I don't know what's happened."

His coffee cup hit the counter hard enough to slosh some of the contents. He snatched up the sponge and swiped at the circle of spilled coffee. "I don't know what's happening either, Laura." His face looked so sad. He turned suddenly and paced to the window, raking a hand through his hair. He muttered an expletive and stalked back to the counter. "Just what I don't need at the moment."

"What is it?" She was bewildered by his sudden irritation this morning and his refusal to look at her.

"We're about to have company," he informed her.

"What?"

"Erin and my brother and his wife. Perfect timing!" He was still glowering at the door when it opened and a man and woman came in, laughing, followed closely by Erin.

"Hey, Laura!" Erin called in obvious delight. "You're here! Great! I was just telling Alan we ought to go pick you up. Good morning, brother. Mmmm. Hope the coffee's strong."

By the time Erin had finished her commentary she had crossed the kitchen to the coffeepot, and

Laura saw that David had had time to wipe all lingering traces of anger from his face. His expression was casual and relaxed, and Laura wondered if anyone else saw the vestiges of some other emotion flickering in his eyes.

"Well, do the introductions, David!" Erin urged her brother as she poured coffee. "By the way, Laura, that sweater never looked so good on me."

Laura felt her face flush. "I was wearing a dress, but . . . since it's snowing . . ." She shrugged lamely, embarrassed at trying to explain why she was wearing Erin's clothes.

But Erin waved away her halting explanation. "I know, I know. David probably told you to dress formally, then decided to build a snowman." She jabbed a finger at David. "Are you going to be a good host or not?"

"If you would let me get a word in edgewise," David told her, crossing his arms and leaning against the counter, "I'd do the introductions. Of course, if you keep chattering away it will be Monday before anybody knows who anybody else is."

Erin pretended to pout, but she winked at Laura as David finally introduced his brother Alan, not quite as tall as David but with the same dark brown hair and engaging smile, and Alan's wife Sonya, a tiny redhead with freckles and sparkling eyes.

"Now what I thought we'd all do today," Erin said, sitting down at the table and propping her feet on the heat register as she outlined her game plan, "is take in a movie and maybe get a pizza." She glanced at Laura and quickly amended, "That is, if a movie's no problem."

"As long as it's not *Bambi*. One thing I can't read are deer lips."

Laura looked at David and found his eyes searching her face, a grim look around his mouth. He looked away quickly and shook his head. "No, we didn't have any plans. Whatever you want to do." Erin apparently didn't notice his lack of enthusiasm and went on with her plans, spreading open the Sunday newspaper and looking over the movie ads with Sonya. Laura looked at David again, but he wouldn't look back, and she felt a growing frustration. *Dammit,* what was wrong?

"Now, ladies," Alan said, biting back a grin. "Before you start setting your taste buds for pizza and popcorn and God knows what else you're going to demand —" The grin broke out now as he ducked the wadded advertisement Erin threw at him. "First, somebody has to clear the drive. We got here in a Jeep, but Grendel's car will slide off the driveway if she tries it."

"That woman drives like Mario Andretti," Sonya conceded, shaking her head. "I've seen cakes she delivered to receptions, and the plastic bride and groom were wearing neck braces because of whiplash."

Laura had missed much of what Sonya said because she wasn't watching her lips early on, but she caught enough to piece it together, and laughed with Erin.

Alan said something, and to her dismay Laura realized she wasn't catching the words. Slowly and quietly she edged away from the table and pretended to refill her cup at the counter. She couldn't hear anything at the table and there was no way she could follow the conversation with lipreading alone. She subtly moved her hand to her right ear and adjusted the controls on the aid.

Fingers brushed her neck, and she turned, startled to see David standing beside her. She saw his lips move. *Are you all right?*

She nodded and turned the gain control. Nothing. She gave him a helpless shrug, staring into his eyes. His fingers stayed there on her shoulder, just a touch, but she sensed that whatever was wrong between them was not so deep that David didn't care about her anymore. And she suddenly knew how important that was to her.

She turned back to the table, able to see the faces there and their lips as they talked. Now they were deciding who would use the tractor with its snow blade to clear the drive. Erin was claiming that she could do it faster than Alan, and they finally settled the issue by flipping a coin. Erin won the toss and surprised them all by magnanimously allowing Alan to do the snow clearing.

"I think I've just been had," Alan complained

155

as Erin tossed him his gloves.

"Come on," David said, clapping him on the shoulder. "We'll do it together."

As he put on his jacket he caught Laura's eye. He stopped with his arm in midair and looked at her hard, and she saw some kind of indecision on his face. Then he shrugged into the jacket and followed Alan out the door.

By the time Laura had helped Sonya and Erin clean up the coffee cups the men had the tractor running and were clearing the drive, David driving and Alan shoveling the walk.

"Come on," Erin said. "Let's go supervise."

She herded the women outside and cupped her hands around her mouth. "You missed a spot!" she called cheerfully, pointing to a clump of snow in the drive.

Laura couldn't hear what David said, but Erin grinned and gave a thumbs-up sign.

"Don't try to tell me how to shovel snow," Alan warned her when she turned to him. "I only take orders from Sonya."

"I do *not* give you orders," Sonya said indignantly.

"Of course not, my sweet," he said, leaning on the shovel and flashing his version of the devilish Evers grin. "You make strong suggestions. You and Erin."

"Now, now, Alan," Erin said, a mischievous light in her own eyes. "You shouldn't insult two sweet, lovely ladies who just happen" — she bent and slowly fashioned a snowball — "to have wonderful throwing arms."

Sonya, grinning now, began making her own snowball. "Oh, dear husband, you are going to be *so* sorry," she said sweetly.

"Oh, yeah?" Alan said, feigning innocence.

"Yeah!" Sonya let her snowball fly, and Alan dodged out of the way, the snow hitting his shoulder and powdering his jacket.

"To the fort!" Erin called. "Come on, Laura! We'll mow 'em down!"

She grabbed Laura's hand and pulled her along until the three of them ducked behind a large evergreen just as a barrage of snowballs sailed past their heads. Laura began forming snowballs and laughing as Erin hurled insults and frozen missiles at Alan, who had now been joined by David. Sonya stood up and fired over the evergreen, hitting Alan solidly in his hair, and all three women whooped victoriously.

"Sonya," Alan called. "This isn't going to look good when our son finds out his old man got clobbered by his mom! Think about his poor little male psyche."

"I think it's *your* little male psyche on the line!" Sonya called back, standing up to fire another snowball. This time Alan was ready and Sonya squealed as a mound of snow exploded on her neck. She plopped back down beside Erin and Laura, sputtering and wiping her jacket.

Laura peered around the bush, and, seeing David kneeling on the snow packing a snowball, she took aim and threw. It was a lucky hit, though she was never going to admit that. Her wobbly throw landed smack on the front of David's jacket and he sat down in surprise.

"Way to go, Laura!" Erin shouted in laughter, giving Laura a hearty thump on her back. The women fell to furiously manufacturing more ammunition, giggling among themselves, and Laura realized how naturally David's family included her in their shenanigans. Her heart clutched at the memory of the children when she returned to school with her bulky hearing aid and how suddenly nobody wanted her on their team for Red Rover or dodge ball. She had proved to the kids that she was just as good as they were, and she had fought in her adult life to prove the same thing to others who should have known better. It was a wonderful feeling not to have to prove anything to anyone in this family.

"It's awfully quiet out there," Erin observed suddenly, frowning. She peered cautiously around the bush. "Uh-oh."

Just as Laura and Sonya leaned forward to see what was wrong, a barrage of snowballs landed on their backs and the two men shouted triumphantly from behind them.

Alan tackled Erin and Sonya at the same time, a slight tactical error as both women managed to pin him down and rub snow on his face. Laura looked over her shoulder in surprise as David swooped down on her, rolling her over onto her back in the snow and straddling her. He was grinning down at her as he traced a line down

158

her nose with a snowy finger and she laughed, wrinkling her nose. "You've fallen in with a bad crowd, kid," he teased her, trying to look stern. "This just won't do at all."

"It won't, huh?"

He shook his head. "Nope. Not at all."

"So what are you going to do about it?" she challenged him, feeling the familiar thready rhythm of her pulse as she looked up into his handsome face.

He picked up a handful of snow and considered it. "Well, I could pay you back for that direct hit and put this cold, *cold* snow down your sweater." One eyebrow rose devilishly. "Or —"

"Or?" she asked, trying not to smile.

He looked into her eyes, and her breath was suspended in her throat. "Or I could do this." His voice trailed off on a husky note, and his mouth came down slowly on hers, so slowly that she was aching for the sweet taste of him for what seemed like hours before his lips brushed hers. His hands cradled her head, holding it off the snow as his mouth thoroughly kissed hers. She found her arms wrapped around his neck somehow, pressing him closer to her.

Laura felt vibrations on the ground and her eyes opened to see Alan thrashing on the ground to the side. "David! Will you quit fooling around and help me!" David was smiling softly, but he moved over beside her on the snow and she sat up. Alan was valiantly trying to hold Sonya and Erin at arm's length and they were trying equally hard to pull up his shirt. "God! I give!" Alan collapsed in a cloud of frosted breath with a long groan. "Vindictive," he said. "That's what you women are." He struggled to a sitting position and pointed a finger at David. "And in my hour of need, where were you?"

"I had my hands full," David said, grinning.

"Yeah, sorta looked that way," Erin said, surveying them with a speculative smile. "So, maybe we should all just go away and leave you two alone." She raised her eyebrows.

"It's all right," David said. "I guess we can stand to be around you for one day anyway."

"Mmm-hmmm," Erin said, and Laura saw that she and David were the object of three pairs of appraising eyes and raised brows.

"Well," David said, clearing his throat to break the silence and pushing himself to his feet. He pulled Laura up with him. "What movie are we going to see?"

"Really, David," Sonya said, trying not to smile. "If you'd rather not go . . ."

"Yeah, brother," Alan said, his grin almost slipping out. "I mean if you have other things you'd rather do, we understand."

Laura dared a glance at David and found him smiling, unperturbed. He looped an arm around her shoulder and said, "Naw. We'll humor you and go to the movie. Somebody has to keep an eye on Erin. You know how loudly she cries in sad movies."

Erin poked him in the arm with her fist as Alan

160

and Sonya laughed. Then it became a game to see who could find the saddest movie to see so Erin would bawl loudly. Finally they all piled into the Jeep, still trying to agree on a movie. Laura was in the back between Erin and David, and she followed the banter the best she could while Erin gave Alan back as good as she got.

David touched Laura's arm and she looked at him. He seemed curiously withdrawn again, as if the interlude in the snow had been a slip of some kind. *Will you be able to hear the movie?* he mouthed.

Laura smiled. "I can usually follow them pretty well," she said softly. "Although subtitles definitely help." He nodded shortly and looked away, leaving Laura to worry again about what was wrong.

Sonya and Alan couldn't decide on a suitably sad current movie so they stopped at a grocery store and took everyone to their house to see a tape of *Dark Victory*. They all sprawled on cushions on the floor in front the TV, and by the end of the tape Erin had fulfilled everyone's expectations by liberally salting her popcorn with her tears. "Oh, God, that was good!" she sniffled, pulling another tissue from the box Alan had set down beside her two hours earlier.

"I see all that boohooing didn't kill your appetite," Alan observed, picking up the last rubbery piece of pepperoni pizza from the greasy cardboard. "Did anybody ever mention that you were adopted into the family, Erin? I mean, we all thought you'd notice that you eat three times the amount of food anyone else in the family consumes, but you know how it is — we didn't want to say anything."

Erin threw a pillow at him in between her dwindling sniffles. "Clod," she said.

David stretched his arms over his head and then looked at his watch. "Artie wants to go over some reports with me this afternoon. I guess Laura and I had better get going." He watched her as she levered herself up from the floor. "Is it all right if I drop you off?" he asked.

There was a formal, distant look on his face, and she strained to catch the sound of his words, to try to pick out some warmth, but her blasted hearing aid wouldn't cooperate. "That would be fine," she answered, trying to look into his eyes, but he wouldn't let her. So she bent and picked up her purse and stood awkwardly while David helped her on with her coat, his fingers not lingering. She thanked his family for the movie and the pizza and then they were walking through the snow. Alan had given David the keys to the Jeep; David had promised to bring it back that night, after his meeting.

Laura had the unsettling feeling that she was being returned home, much the same as the Jeep would be returned to Alan that night. David's unnatural quietness and emotional retreat were driving her crazy. Other than what had happened during the snowball fight, he'd hardly looked at her all day. It was almost as if . . .

As if she had trespassed by making love to him in his house, in *Barbara*'s house. The simple explanation left her reeling. He hadn't let go of the past after all. She had committed the sin of loving him in the bed where his wife should have been. She turned her face to the window to hide the sudden blur of tears. *So what did you expect, Kincaid?* she chided herself. *You walked into this with your eyes open.*

At her apartment he helped her out of the car and walked her to her door. Then he just leaned against it with his hands jammed into his pockets. "Could I come by to see you tomorrow night?" he asked.

She was so surprised she said, "What?"

"I'm afraid it will be late, but if you could —"

So what was he going to do, she wondered vaguely, be the perfect gentleman and give her a list of reasons why this wouldn't work?

She pushed open the door and bent to scratch an enthusiastically welcoming Horton's ears. "I guess so," she said.

"I'll be by later then," he said. "You won't forget, will you?"

"No. Will you?"

He sighed. "No . . . We'll talk, Laura."

"He says we'll talk," she informed Horton later that night as she got ready to climb into bed. "I think it's the big good-bye, Horton. What do you think?" She lay down on the bed, enveloped in silence, and stared at the ceiling.

He was right about one thing. It was indeed late when he came by her apartment the next night. She had almost given up on seeing him by nine, and she had changed from her skirt and blouse to a pair of jeans and an oversized sweat shirt.

"I'm sorry," he said when she opened the door. "I tried to get away earlier." He shrugged and ran a hand through his hair.

She could see the exhaustion around his eyes and mouth, and she shook her head. "It's all right. Come on in."

She hung up his coat, looking back over her shoulder as he sank onto her couch and leaned his head back, eyes closed. "I have hot water ready. Do you want some tea?"

"Yes . . . please."

She thought he might be asleep when she set the tea down in front of him, but without opening his eyes he said, "How was your day?"

"It was all right." She had gone to the Hastings Institute that afternoon, and again Anne had urged her to consider taking the position of assistant director. Clara had had a bad day too, and Laura had come home discouraged.

He reached out and touched her hand to get her attention. "No, it wasn't, was it?"

"No," she agreed softly. "It wasn't."

"Mine was hell too, in case you want to know."

She stood there looking at him and trying to decipher the sadness she saw in his eyes. "What's wrong, David?" she asked, steeling herself.

"Come here," he said, holding out his hand.

She placed her fingers on his larger, rougher ones and came around the coffee table to sit down beside him. He turned his head where it lay on the back of the couch and studied her, his fingers lightly stroking her hand as it lay between them.

"I found out today I'm not getting an endorsement I'd counted on, and then Artie got overenthusiastic and booked me to speak to two gardening clubs on the same night when I don't know a rose from a rutabaga." He smiled grimly. "And the computers went down three times at the paper today." He closed his eyes again and heaved a sigh, and the silence lengthened. "But the thing that bothers me most about this whole weekend," he said, his voice so quiet that she had to read his lips, "is that you didn't trust me, Laura."

She stared at him as he opened his eyes. He looked tired — and angry. "I don't know what you mean," she said uncertainly.

"I know about the Fielding School for the Deaf and Buddy Fielding — and Lori Fielding."

Her blood froze. For all of her dread, when he finally found out it caught her completely off guard. "How — how did you find out?" she asked hesitantly.

"I made the connection the night before last when you were signing in your sleep. Something about you was so familiar, and it all sort of clicked into place."

His fingers still gripped hers, but she felt numb. She looked away from him, focusing on the other side of the room, trying to distance herself from the choking feeling inside her chest. His hand brushed her chin and turned her face back to his.

"Why didn't you tell me, Laura?" And now she saw it in his face, the pain he'd concealed from her since that night. "What in God's name did you think I'd do that would be so awful?"

"Never see me again," she said quietly and succinctly, looking into his eyes and showing him her own pain.

He shook his head. "Why would you think I'd do that?" He was truly baffled. "None of what happened was your fault. It's in the past now anyway. It doesn't matter anymore."

"Doesn't matter?" She gave a short laugh. "David, I don't come from your world. I don't have a sterling background or a supportive family. What I have is an ex-husband named Buddy Fielding who swindled a lot of nice people. And, like it or not, I'm associated with that swindle."

"Laura, you're talking like you're tainted or something," he said, pushing to his feet in agitation and pacing.

"Listen to me, David!" Her hands were clenched at her sides. "I'm not a naive girl anymore. I know what even a hint of scandal can do to a political career. I refuse to ruin something good in your life!"

He stopped and faced her, his eyes a stormy gray blue. "If that's how you feel, then I'll drop out of the race," he said quietly.

"No!" She stood up now and faced him angrily. "I won't let you throw away something important!"

"Laura, for God's sake, listen to me!" He crossed to her and grasped her shoulders. "I don't want to have to choose between you and the state senate, but if it comes down to that — then hell, it's no contest. You're far more important to me, Laura. Far more." She could feel his hands trembling on her shoulders despite the pressure. "Don't you know that?" His eyes pierced hers in desperation. "Dammit, Laura, don't you know what you mean to me? For the first time in ages I feel alive again." He gave a dry laugh. "Even Artie, who has tunnel vision when it comes to anything but campaigning, noticed the change in me. That's you, Laura. That's what he saw. And don't say you don't care for me. Because I won't buy that."

She could feel tears gathering in the corners of her eyes, but she wouldn't let them fall. "*Care* for you? David Evers, it's because I care for — no, dammit, *love* you! — that I don't want to ruin your career. I — didn't do Buddy any good, and before you say anything" — she held up her hands — "I know that wasn't my fault. But I don't think I could go through that again. Because I know what kind of man you are. And you'd put on a brave face and tell me everything was just fine and then you'd stick it out no matter how miserable you were."

"Laura, I'm not Buddy!"

"Oh, hell, David, don't you think I know that? Why do you think it matters so much to me that you not get hurt? And why the hell do you think I keep comparing myself to Barbara?"

She didn't know the tears had escaped until she found David's arms around her, pressing her to his chest. "Don't cry, baby," he said with a groan. "Don't cry. It isn't so bad. Come on, honey."

She sensed what he was saying by the cadence of the murmurings she felt in his chest as he sat down and pulled her onto his lap. His hand smoothed her hair in a ceaseless, comforting motion. She kept on crying, for him and for herself and for the love she felt for him.

When her sobs subsided to snuffles, he put gentle fingers beneath her chin and raised her face to his. "All through?"

She nodded and then fresh tears started. "Oh, dammit, David," she said. "I kept putting off telling you, because I just couldn't find the words and then" — she stopped crying long enough to blow her nose in the handkerchief David handed her — "and then you find out, and I tell you we can't go on seeing each other — and then you try to talk me out of breaking it off."

She snuffled loudly. "I don't understand this relationship, David."

She could feel the chuckle start in his chest, and she began to smile herself. The chuckle erupted into a laugh, and Laura pressed her arms around his neck, laughing now as hard as she had been crying just a few minutes before, clinging to him as he rocked with mirth.

"You're a typical woman, Laura Kincaid, you know that?" he teased her when they'd both caught their breath.

"A typical woman!" she repeated. She released him to wipe her eyes with the backs of her hands, then looked at him and with a sly smile held each hand with two fingers extended and brought her hands together and then apart.

"And what's that mean?" he asked.

Her smile broadened. "Politely put, it means buzz off."

"And not so politely?" he said with raised brows.

Laura grinned, and he nodded. "Yeah, I thought that's what it meant," he said ruefully. "If we're going to communicate I think you're going to have to teach me some of your language. Now don't laugh. And you can start with something nice and clean." His own smile grew as he looked at her. "Aw, hell, forget nice and clean. Teach me the good stuff first."

"Oh, sure, get me to lead you astray."

"How do you say this?" he murmured, brushing his lips over hers, making her light-headed with the sensations that sprang to life inside her. "Show me," he said, lifting his head.

Smiling quietly, her eyes on his, Laura held both her hands up and touched the fingers and thumbs at one point.

"Kiss," he said, imitating the way she held her hands. "Now show me *love*."

She couldn't take her eyes from his face, from the way he watched her — blue eyes holding her in thrall — and the way his breathing grew erratic just from a mere gesture she made. Slowly again, she curled her fingers inward and held her arms against her chest, crossed at the wrists. *Love,* she mouthed.

"Love," he repeated, imitating her action. His gaze held hers, and she could feel so many emotions welling up inside her that she wanted to cry. *Oh, David, what I feel for you . . .*

"It's beautiful the way you say it — with your hands," he said, holding her away from him and smiling. And then he pointed to himself, crossed his wrists over his chest and pointed to her. *I love you.*

She closed her eyes as he took her into his arms. It would work, she told herself. They would make it work.

Chapter 8

And the bug said, "Wow! You have wings! Pretty wings!" The butterfly said, "You mean I'm not ugly anymore?" "Oh, no," said the bug. "You're the most beautiful thing I ever saw."

Laura was telling the story in sign language to a class at the Hastings Institute, stopping occasionally to sign a child's name in the audience and ask a question about the story. Each child eagerly signed the answer. They caught on to this quickly, more quickly than many did to the laborious task of picking out sounds with their hearing aids. The children who could even wear aids, that is. Some of these kids in front of her had no residual hearing at all and were totally deaf. They made friends among themselves quickly though, and they took to signing enthusiastically.

Their animated faces lit up with laughter when she made the sign for the bug. It was one of the first signs Laura had learned herself, and she loved making a face as she held her crossed hands to her face, her thumbs touching her nose and her first two fingers extended. She went on with the story of the bug and the butterfly, slowing herself down so the children could follow her signs. *And the beautiful butterfly flew to a flower and drank its nectar. "You liked me when I was ugly," the butterfly said. "And now that I'm beautiful you're my favorite flower."* Laura looked around at the circle of rapt faces. *And each of you is beautiful, like the butterfly,* she signed. *Say it with me — I am beautiful.*

The children repeated the sign and beamed at Laura. From the corner of her eye Laura saw the light come on signaling the end of class. The children were gathering their books and Laura dismissed them.

Julie touched her arm, and when Laura looked at her she said, "Why the frown? You did a fantastic job. They didn't move an inch during the whole story."

Laura nodded wearily. "Thanks. It's this stupid thing." She tapped her ear. "I've got to get it checked."

"Listen, thanks again for taking over this hour for me."

"No problem. I enjoyed it."

Julie gave Laura a smile and looked pointedly toward the door. Laura followed her gaze and stared in surprise at David standing just inside the door. Beside him was Anne Tyler.

Julie tapped Laura's arm. "I'll see you later."

Laura nodded and smiled at David. She hadn't seen him all week, not since the night at her apartment when he told her he knew who she was. "Hi," she said softly.

"Hi," he said, and she loved the grin of pure

pleasure he had just from seeing her.

"How long have you been here?" she asked.

"Oh, ten minutes or so," he said. "I ran into Mrs. Tyler in the hall and we talked a while before we got caught up in watching you through the door." He shook his head in awe. "Watching you sign is like watching a ballet dancer. It's that beautiful."

"I told David I've been trying to talk you into taking the assistant directorship," Anne said. "He agrees with me."

"He's a little prejudiced," Laura said in a loud whisper, leaning toward Anne as if David couldn't hear.

Anne laughed. "Never mind that. Here, I brought you this brochure from the college. It lists all the classes for next fall, and it looks to me like you could get your master's in three semesters. You'd be done about the time I plan to resign as director. And in the meantime you could fill in as assistant director while you're going to school."

"Why do I get the feeling I'm being railroaded here?" Laura said.

"Just think about it," Anne said, putting a hand on her arm. "You'd do wonders for this school."

When Anne was gone, Laura looked at David with a wry lift of her eyebrows. "Why not?" she said lightly. "I did wonders for this school before. Not many people could have managed to close it single-handedly."

David put his hands on her upper arms and looked into her face. "Don't, Laura," he said. "Don't even think like that. Anne's right. You'd be perfect for the job."

She stared at him soberly. "I don't want to hurt these kids, David. And . . . I don't want to hurt you either."

"Hey!" he said, lightly punching her arm. "This is me you're talking to here. I'm running for public office. I've got a hide like an armadillo. Now come on. The armadillo is going to cook you dinner."

"What do armadillos eat, anyway?" she asked on the way out.

"I don't know. Bugs or something." He put his arm around her shoulders and pulled her to him as they walked. "But I promise not to make anything that will make you go 'yuck' tonight," he said, bending to look into her face.

Whenever he looked at her like that she could feel her pulse speed, her blood grow heavy with desire. At the slightest touch she wanted him. At the merest memory of him, maybe catching a hint of the scent of his soap on someone else or catching a glimpse of a man in a crowd whose hair was almost his shade — the smallest reminder and her knees would grow suddenly wobbly and her stomach would clutch in anticipation.

"Laura," he said, touching her arm as they reached his car. She stopped and looked up at him. "I need to drop by someone's house on the way. The guy is doing a lot of campaign work for me in his area. He — well, he lives near where you grew up, Laura. In Larson. I read that in the clipping about you and Buddy — that you were from Larson." Gently he brushed back a piece of her hair that the wind had blown across her cheek. "He publishes the newspaper there. Do you mind? I can call him if you'd rather not go."

She stared over his shoulder at the gray clouds gathering on the horizon, trying to make up her mind. She knew what he was telling her — there was a good chance the newspaper publisher would know who she was. This was what she had hated after the scandal at the Fielding School, the questions, the publicity, the way she was forced into the public eye whether she wanted it or not. But David was giving her a choice. She remembered the iron bridge and how she had felt when she finally got the courage to stand in the middle of it again.

"All right," she said, opening the passenger door. "Let's go."

David smiled. "Have I ever told you you're something else, Laura Kincaid?"

"Yeah, well, just don't get specific about exactly what it is I am," she said gruffly to cover the flutterings of her heart at David's nearness as he leaned in the car to give her a brief kiss on the nose before he closed the car door. *I'd walk across hot coals for him,* she told herself as he settled in beside her. *Which is darn close to what I'm about to do.*

He asked her questions about the Hastings Institute as he drove, and he seemed concerned about Clara. "Why is it so important that such a little girl learn to use a hearing aid now?" he asked.

"It's easier for her to make the adjustment now while she's young. She'll learn to speak much more clearly if she can hear some sound."

"But can't she communicate with sign language?"

Laura gave him a tired smile. "Sure — but with how many people? It may not be entirely fair, but the world is for those who hear. It's very difficult to get along if you can't speak. Or lipread," she added.

They drove in silence a while longer, and she could tell from the intent way he stared straight ahead that something was on his mind. Finally he broached the subject.

"Laura, do you like what you do at the Hastings Institute?"

It came out of the blue, and she gave him an honest answer. "Yes, I love it. Why?"

"Because Anne's right. You'd be a wonderful director. Assistant director first."

"David," she said wearily. "We've been over this. I'd love the job, I truly would. But it's because I love that place so much that I'm not going to risk giving it bad publicity. What if someone like Clara's mother reacted negatively to . . . Lori Fielding —" She stumbled over the words, and David interrupted.

176

"You're not Lori Fielding anymore, Laura."

"But I *was* once, David. And what if Clara's mother took her out of the school because of me? I couldn't stand that."

"And what if two or three other kids dropped out after Anne leaves because they don't like some other new director?" he said impatiently. "There are too many *ifs* in life. You of all people should know that."

They sat in strained silence, and then she said, "I'll think about it, David. That's as far as I can go right now."

He placed his hand over hers. "All right. That's all I ask of anything, Laura. Just give it a chance."

She knew he was talking about more than just the job, and she stared out the window at the washed-out pink of the sunset and the low-hanging gray clouds. There was still snow on the ground, although here in the city it was gray and slushy with footprints. She was glad it would be dark when they drove into Larson. She felt all raw inside now, and seeing everything in the harsh light of day would be like running hot water on that rawness.

She noticed when they passed the city limits, and she couldn't help the sudden surge of adrenaline as she recognized familiar landmarks, but she kept her eyes resolutely ahead and didn't say anything. When David stopped the car in front of a white bungalow with two big trees out front she looked around and saw that they were only a quarter mile from the house where she grew up. A lot of old emotions came rushing back, but she resolutely got out of the car and lifted her chin as he took her arm and led her toward the door.

The porch light was on, and a short, balding man with a portly belly straining the buttons of his white shirt opened the door. His shirt sleeves were rolled up, revealing hairy arms, and he pumped David's hand enthusiastically. Laura recognized him before she was introduced.

"Bob, this is Laura Kincaid," David said, standing aside to let Laura enter first. "Laura, Bob Randall is an old friend and a good newspaperman."

"It's nice to meet you, Mr. Randall," Laura said, shaking his hand. "I used to read your paper all the time."

Bob Randall looked at her quizzically. "Just call me Bob," he told her. "Come on in and sit down. I'll get those volunteer lists and canvassing reports for you, David."

Laura and David sat on the couch in the living room, and David squeezed her hand. "We won't stay long," he promised her.

When Bob came back he handed David a sheaf of papers and gave him an apologetic grin. "Your workers have been busy. The second page has a list of responses we got to that letter stating your position on a state income tax increase. We included a copy of my editorial along with it."

"You're doing a great job, Bob," David said appreciatively.

"Yeah, well, maybe in exchange you can give me some advice on that nephew of mine. He says he wants a position where he can help the under-privileged but still afford a Porsche and vacations in Europe." Bob winked at Laura. "I tell him he's a hipyup — half-hippie, half-yuppie." He leaned back and settled his eyes on Laura as their laughter filled the room. Bob sighed. "Seriously, I sometimes wonder where old-fashioned values have gone. Money is the big lure these days, the making of it, the investing of it to make more, the spending of it." He leaned forward and added ruefully, "There I go with my soap-box speech. I guess I'm showing my age. Have to tell the young people how to run the country. It's an occupational disease of old newspapermen."

"I remember something you said a long time ago," Laura said hesitantly. "You told a group of kids that they had their whole lives ahead of them and that there was no one right path to take. 'You'll find many roads in your future,' you said. You said to always take the most scenic one and savor the journey, even if the path wasn't strewn with money. Life isn't meant to be lived wearing blinders. The richest, fullest life is the one that's spent looking." She gave a self-conscious smile. "I'm paraphrasing. You were much more eloquent."

Bob sat up, looking astounded. "Now how on earth did you remember that?" he asked. "Let's see now. When did I give that speech?"

"It was twelve years ago. You spoke to my high

school graduating class." Laura hesitated, then said, "I was sitting on the stage behind you." She pointed to her hearing aid and smiled. "I couldn't hear very well from behind you, so I bought the newspaper the next day. It carried the full text of your speech."

"Twelve years ago," Bob said in wonder. "I remember that speech now. So you were one of those bright kids on the stage." He frowned. "Laura Kincaid. You grew up here?"

She hesitated only a split second, her eyes looking for David's and meeting briefly. "Yes, I grew up here."

"What did you do after graduation?" Bob asked.

Laura brushed back her hair and saw Bob's eyes go to the hearing aid. "I was involved with the Fielding School for the Deaf," she said simply. "I was married to Buddy Fielding."

She felt David's hand lightly touching her back, and she was grateful for his quiet support. "It was a long time ago," David said.

"My gosh," Bob said in surprise. "I'd almost forgotten about — all that. But you weren't called 'Laura' then, were you?"

She shook her head. "Buddy preferred to call me 'Lori.' "

"Lori Fielding," he said slowly. "Yes, now I remember. What have you been doing since" — he coughed discreetly — "since the school reopened under new management?"

Laura smiled wryly. "I've been working as a

photographer at *Springfield Today,* and I've been back at Hastings as a volunteer."

Bob sat back and rested his hands on his knees as he studied Laura. "You know," he said, "I remember that afternoon when you and your husband held the press conference to announce that you were leaving the school. The investors had already told the newspapers about the financial problems. And I looked at you up there beside Buddy Fielding, and I thought to myself, 'How did an intelligent, sensitive woman like that get hooked up with that man?' I think a lot of us there that day wondered the same thing."

He glanced at David, and David's fingers gently stroked Laura's back. Laura looked down at her hands and then back to Bob. "I wasn't much more than a child when I met him, and in the beginning anyway he really seemed to care about other people." She frowned and shrugged. "But things change. I think it was when his brother died that he started craving money the way a child craves food. He was an insecure man, and his father fed those insecurities, always comparing him unfavorably to his brother. After Buddy's brother died his father wouldn't stop grieving or wishing out loud that it had been Buddy instead." She looked down at her hands again. "That can do something to a man."

The room fell quiet, and Laura watched Bob's face and saw the understanding there — and something that looked like admiration. "If you don't mind my asking," he said hesitantly, "how did you two meet?"

"I did some photographs of his house for *Springfield Today*," Laura said.

She looked at David, and he smiled. "And we've been together ever since, as the cliché goes," David said.

"I see," Bob said, looking from one to the other. "Listen, I know this may be uncomfortable for you, Laura, but — well, I can't help it. Yours is a great story, I mean, how your life has changed, how the Hastings Institute is doing now. I'd really like to write about it if you'd let me."

Laura squared her shoulders and looked him in the eye. "I wouldn't mind. It's time I put the past in perspective."

"Great! How about now? Just relax and let me get us some coffee." He leaped to his feet and then looked at them anxiously. "It's not too late tonight, is it? I mean, I hate to put this off when I'm so all fired up about it."

Laura laughed. "No, go ahead."

David groaned. "You're ruining my social life, Bob. You know that, don't you?"

"Hell, David, if I can't ruin yours, whose can I ruin?" He grinned and left the room, and David turned Laura's face toward his.

"Are you sure you want to do this?" Blue eyes probed hers, and she met them frankly. "It's all right?" he asked.

"I'm scared," she admitted, "but it's time. It

— doesn't hurt to think about it as much as it used to."

"I wish it didn't hurt at all," he said gravely, pulling her to him for a fierce hug. "I wish to hell I could just fix things for you."

He released her and she smiled up at him. "You could start with this thing," she said, tapping her ear piece.

"You're having trouble?" He frowned.

"I seem to be missing an awful lot lately." She shrugged. "I've got an appointment with my doctor next week. I'll get it checked then."

He started to say something else, but Bob returned. Laura could feel David's worry and she pressed his hand to reassure him.

The stars were out when they left Bob's house, and Laura stared at them through the window as they drove slowly away. She felt exhausted but somehow cleansed, as though the weight of her past had been finally lifted from her shoulders by the simple act of telling someone else her story. David had listened attentively while she talked, and occasionally she had seen a flash of anger on his face when she spoke of Buddy. He hadn't said anything since they'd said good night to Bob.

Laura wasn't paying any attention to where they were going until a familiar store sign caught her eye. She grasped David's arm and said, "That's where I used to live."

He pulled the car over to the curb, and even

before it had fully stopped she was opening the door and jumping out. It was a still, crisp night, and she jammed her hands in her coat pockets as she stared up at the tiny apartment above the drugstore, a lone light burning in one window.

David came up behind her, and she felt his hands touch her upper arms, but she didn't turn around. "We lived there," she said, pointing to the apartment. "That light is in the kitchen. My mother used to have her sewing machine in the corner there and she'd make my dresses. She'd sew for other women too, to make extra money. She was so proud of me when I graduated from high school as an honors student and I sat on the stage —" Her voice broke and she bit back tears. David leaned forward, his hands stroking her arms through the coat, a gesture of futile comforting. She felt his breath against her neck, and she knew he'd said something, but she'd heard nothing, only felt the warmth of his mouth. From this perspective, she could see that the apartment was even tinier than she'd remembered: the street-level wooden door that led to the stairs was shabby and unpainted.

"I brought my friends home to that apartment," she said quietly, "and my mother loved that. She wanted more than anything for me to have friends. And one day I brought Marie Fessler home. She had to pick up a prescription at the drugstore, and I invited her up for a soda." Laura fell silent a moment, not even feeling David's hands gripping her arms. "Mom splurged two weeks later and gave me a birthday party — a cake, favors, ice cream, the whole thing. And she told me to invite all my friends. I sent out the invitations, and the next day in school Marie told me she couldn't come. 'I saw a bug on your stairs,' she said. 'My mother says your mother isn't clean.' Do you know that what she said about my mother hurt me more than anything anyone has ever said about my being deaf?" She crossed her arms suddenly and fiercely. "I told Mom Marie had to go to the doctor that day."

David turned her around gently but firmly, and his eyes seemed to blaze in the darkness. He carefully wiped her cheeks with his thumbs and she realized then that she was crying. "It doesn't matter," she said to him. "It was so long ago."

"It matters to me," he said. "I'm in love with the woman who was the little girl up there." He nodded his head toward the light in the window. "I'd give anything to be able to go back in time and protect her from those hurts — and to thank her mother for the woman she turned out to be." He lowered his forehead until it touched hers. "Sometimes it's so hard for me not to fight your battles for you. Half of me wanted to take your hand and pull you right out of Bob's house so you wouldn't have to tell him all that. But I knew you were doing what you had to do, honey. And it's hard."

"Yes," she agreed. "It's hard." She let her eyes drift closed, trying to summon up her childhood here. The thumping she could feel through the

185

floor when someone banged the drugstore door, the heat rising from the pavement in the summer, the smell of onions cooking in the Italian restaurant two doors down. It was winter she'd liked best here though, because then the whole block had seemed cloaked in silence — at least at twilight and in the early morning — and she'd felt then that the rest of the world was living in her own silent world. She opened her eyes and smiled at David.

"What about your father?" David asked gently.

Laura sighed, remembering vague shadows from childhood. "He wasn't around much," she said, "which was probably a blessing, because all I remember about when he was home is my parents fighting. He fancied himself an entrepreneur and he was always traveling around trying to set up deals." She shrugged, loving the feel of David close to her on this cold, starry night. "He'd buy a little storefront in some town and try to get some kind of a business going, a florist shop or a bakery or something else — it didn't matter what it was — and it always failed. He had grandiose schemes, but no head for business." *He was a lot like Buddy.*

David's fingers brushed her cheeks, his eyes caressing. "Show me the rest of your town," he said. "I want to know everything about you."

"Two blocks will just about cover it," she assured him, smiling now as she took his hand and led him down the street. She pointed in the

186

drugstore window to the rack of comic books, placing her hand over her heart in a parody of breathlessness as she told him how she would wait for the newest Nancy and Sluggo comics and ogle the latest nail polish colors at the same time.

The stores were closed except for the tavern on the corner where a neon beer sign glowed in the window. Laura showed him the Italian restaurant where she would press her nose against the window and try to watch Mr. Angeletti toss his pizza dough high into the air. And then there was the laundromat where she would run with her coins to get a soda from the machine or a candy bar.

She laughed as she pointed out the barber shop where she got her first haircut. "I sat on a board across the chair's arms," she told him. "And the barber gave me a lollipop when he was done. I'd kept my eyes shut during the whole thing, but then I opened them and looked in the mirror and started crying because my long hair was all gone."

She was still laughing as she pulled him on down the street. "The movie theater!" he called as they halted beneath the marquee. "I bet this is where you first held hands."

"And spilled a box of popcorn on his lap," she said.

"And what did he do?"

Laura tilted her head to one side and tried not to smile. "He kissed me."

"What! Why, I ought to punch the fresh twerp," he teased her. "So, how do I compare?" he asked her, eyebrows raised.

"How do you compare?" she repeated, laughing.

"Yeah. Side by side with the twerp?"

"Well, I'm not sure," she said, teasing him in turn. "He had braces at the time and when he went to whisper something in my ear he got hung up on my hearing aid cord."

"So he was a real smooth operator, huh?" David clucked and shook his head. "Well, let's see if I can do better." Laura stood with her head cocked, a smile playing around her mouth as he moved within inches of her and put his hands on her shoulders. The streetlight reflected in his eyes, making them glow like blue sparks. He was wearing his camel-colored coat and she could smell the clean, soapy scent that was his as well as the faint smoky smell of the many places he'd campaigned.

Gentle fingers beneath her chin tilted her head back, and she looked at the millions of stars a second before his head blotted them out and his mouth covered hers. And she wasn't on her hometown street anymore but in some sweet oblivion where only she and David existed. His lips teased and caressed and finally possessed hers with all of his strength and need. Arching against him, her hand finding a thin space to rest between their bodies, Laura could feel her heartbeat drumming inside and his own matching it, two cadences of desire so insistent that they threatened to overwhelm her.

His head raised a fraction, and she looked into those blue eyes awash with desire and vibrant with life, and she loved him so much that it was almost a physical pain. She shifted her body closer to his, pressing against him, and he smiled shakily, trailing one knuckle down her cheek. "You make me forget we're standing on the street," he whispered. "I could make love to you right here." He rubbed her nose with his. "And I could get us both arrested."

Laura grinned. "Then we'd better get on with the tour. Let's go. I want to show you something."

They raced back to the car, laughing, and she gave him directions out of town. Along the way she pointed out her grade school and the cemetery where her mother was buried. "Here!" she cried when they'd gone about a mile. "Pull over here!"

He gave her a quizzical glance. "Right here? On the side of the road?"

She nodded quickly and pointed. "*That's* what I want you to see."

She watched his face register more confusion as he looked ahead. "A bridge?"

Laura nodded. "Come on."

She ran ahead of him, feeling the cold air on her face and an incredible sense of freedom. The bridge loomed starkly in the night, a maze of metal and wood only dimly lit by starlight. Laura didn't hesitate, just ran to the center of the bridge and placed her hands on the railing to stare down into the water. She could make out tiny eddies of reflected light, but she couldn't hear the water at all.

He caught up with her and leaned his forearms on the railing as he stared down into the creek below. They were both silent, and then Laura turned to him and told him about the bridge and how her mother had talked her into walking onto it again. "It was such a small thing," she marveled, "learning to do something that was so easy before. But it was so hard to just . . . do it. My mother knew a lot about people." She frowned and looked down at the water again. "I guess she didn't know so much about my father though — before she married him."

She could feel the thrumming of the iron through her fingers as the wind blew, but she couldn't hear the high-pitched whine it made, a sound she remembered from childhood, before the meningitis. You went through life losing some things, she thought, but you gained others.

David touched her hand and she looked at him. "You didn't know so much about Buddy before you married him either, did you?"

She stared down at her hands a moment, trying to sort it out. Had she known him or had she only thought she did? She finally gave a resigned shrug and shook her head. "Who can say? Sometimes people change for reasons of their own. Sometimes they just get tired of trying to cope."

"He seemed like a desperate, hunted man that day at the press conference. As though he couldn't help what he'd done and he couldn't feel any remorse for it either."

"I don't think he could help it," Laura agreed. "I think he genuinely wanted to start a good school for the deaf — when we were first married. I'd tried a semester at college, but I was too stubborn then to admit I had to make concessions to my hearing problem. I wouldn't ask for a front row seat where I could lipread and consequently I missed most of the lecture." She smiled wryly and pointed to her head. "Bright move on my part, right? Well, anyway, I was flunking three out of four subjects and I still wouldn't tell the teachers I needed some extra help getting the lectures. One day I wandered over to a little hamburger shack off campus where they had a live band. It played loud — so loud that I could hear some of the music and the rest I could feel through the table vibrations." She turned around and leaned her back against the railing, staring up at the stars. "I met Buddy there. He'd dropped out of school and had these wonderful-sounding plans to travel around the country with a band — he would write the music — and then open his own recording studio. Buddy's pipe dream."

She glanced at David, and he said, "Like your father."

Slowly she nodded. "Yes. I guess I was going to prove that I could settle down the man who wouldn't settle down."

"And the band didn't materialize?" he asked, his eyes probing her face.

"Oh, he got his band started all right. And they even played a few gigs. Buddy was the drummer as well as the songwriter. And we got married. I dropped out of school. But — I don't know." She raised her hands helplessly. "He said the band wasn't working out and he needed to do something else. Something 'more challenging.' And then he got on his kick about a school for the deaf."

"I take it he recruited you for that from the beginning," David said dryly.

"Oh, yes. I was his big drawing card for raising funds." She raised a hand as if to brush that thought aside. "Things actually went well until his brother John died. Then it was as if all those years of John coming first in his father's heart, of John being held up as an example, came crashing down on Buddy's head. I was there the night Buddy's father took that one step too far and said he wished it had been Buddy and not John who was killed in the car crash." She closed her eyes and shuddered.

"That can kill a person inside," David allowed when she looked at him.

"It was devastating to Buddy. I think for a while he wished he *had* been the one who died. The school was started by now. He'd rented a large building that used to house an elementary school before the district ran into a decreasing

192

student population. And he was raising money and hiring teachers. But then —" She shook her head. "He was trying to prove to his father that he was as good as John — I guess he was trying to earn his father's love. He started using the school's money for a big house for us and for a swimming pool and cars and vacations. I tried to ask him about it, but he always had a ready explanation. 'This house will be the school's offices soon,' he'd tell me. Or 'The kids will be able to use the pool for phys. ed. classes.' Buddy had a degree in psychology — and he could be charming. Look at all the money he raised. He could make people believe in him."

"Until things came crashing down around him."

Laura stared off into the distance. "We were in Mexico — on one of Buddy's famous 'vacation fund-raisers.' That meant we partied all day and Buddy charmed wealthy investors at night. Word came that one of the investors back home — Ralph Harvey — was calling for an investigation into how the school's money was being spent."

He touched her arm and she looked at him. "I wondered the other night why you seemed so upset at the speech," he said. "I figured out later it was seeing Ralph Harvey."

"Talk about bolts from the blue," Laura said wryly. "Everything came flooding back when I saw him — all the publicity and the shame I felt and the . . . the way I felt about Buddy."

He looked into her face, his eyes seeming to draw out her soul. "How did you feel about him, Laura?" Was that anger in his voice? she wondered.

"I felt betrayed," she said simply. "I'd trusted him. I'd believed him. I'd even tried to change for him, only I couldn't, and I guess he couldn't live with that either."

"Change for him how?" he asked, frowning.

"It was nothing," Laura said, looking away. "He hated the sounds I — never mind, it was nothing." She stared down at the wooden planks, her hands balled into fists in her pockets.

Firm fingers lifted her chin, and she looked into David's eyes. They were a cloudy blue gray, as though he was suffused with some strong emotion. "What sounds, Laura? What was it Buddy said?" His eyes were relentless, seeking hers and probing.

She took a deep breath. She couldn't seem to meet his eyes as she told him. "He said — he was angry — he said that no man —"

"What, Laura?" David said. "No man what?"

It came out in a rush that seemed to pull her insides with it. "No man wants to make love to a woman who can't understand a damn thing he says unless she's staring at his face." She suddenly felt drained of all emotion and she sagged back against the bridge railing. "He hated the sounds I made when we made love," she said in a low voice.

"The damned jackass!" David said savagely.

194

"How could he do that to you?" He gathered Laura into his arms and leaned back against the bridge, cradling her between his legs, as if to shield her from all the bad memories. She could feel him talking and from the brusque movement of his chest she guessed he was calling Buddy a few more choice words, but it was enough for her to be held like this. David's arms were her shelter, and past pain couldn't touch her here.

He brought his head down so she could read his lips. "You're one hell of a woman, Laura, and all the Buddy Fieldings in the world can't take that away from you." Seeing his expression, she guessed at the force of emotion behind his words. "If I could wipe out everything he ever said to you I'd do it no matter what it took. But I can't. So I promise you I'll do the next best thing — I'll be there to share the hurt with you."

"David," she murmured, placing a caressing finger over his lips. "It never hurts when I'm with you. You know that, don't you?" It was important to her that he know, because she regretted the things she'd never told her mother and she was determined not to regret anything with David.

"No," he said softly against her finger, the tightness around his mouth easing. "No, but you don't know how much better I feel hearing you say it." His mouth crooked in the beginning of a shaky smile. "In that case, I'm never leaving your side."

He was kissing her when she felt the rumble of

195

the boards beneath her feet, and they both looked up. A battered pickup truck slowed to a stop beside them and a middle-aged man with a baseball cap leaned toward the passenger window and said something. It was too dark to read his lips and Laura didn't understand what he said. David answered, and the man smiled and touched his fingers to his cap in a salute before he drove off.

"What did he say?" she asked David.

He grinned. "He wanted to know if we were in trouble. I told him no, and he said I would be if I let a pretty one like you get away."

Laura punched his arm lightly. "He didn't say that!"

"Sure he did!" he assured her, still grinning as he put his arm around her shoulders and led her back toward the car.

"Come on, David!" she insisted, and they giggled and teasingly punched each other's arms until they were settled in the car again and on their way.

She loved this man and for completely different reasons than she'd thought she loved Buddy Fielding. She'd believed herself in love with Buddy, when she was really infatuated with the things he was and she thought she was not — competent, secure, self-confident. She loved David for himself, for the man who was boy enough to sometimes eat ice cream for dinner and who mischievously threw snowballs and kissed her in the snow. She loved David because she could be herself with him and he loved her back.

She glanced at him as he drove and he looked over at her and grinned. "I know it's late, but let's go to the cabin anyway. I want to build a fire tonight."

"A big fire?" she teased him.

"A raging fire," he answered with a crooked, devilish smile, and though she couldn't hear his words she saw the seductive embers in his eyes. And she added one more thing to the list of reasons why she loved David Evers.

Chapter 9

David surprised Laura by appearing at her office the next afternoon, perching one hip on her desk and provoking a flurry of tie straightening and throat clearing by the rest of the staff. "Do you have any plans after work?" he asked, his eyes an open declaration of desire that made Laura feel as though the office furnace, normally offering only sporadic heat, had suddenly rejuvenated itself and elevated the temperature to the degree that Katrina's miniskirt warranted.

Laura smiled and shook her head. "Ice cream?" she asked hopefully.

David rolled his eyes. "That could be arranged."

"Well, in that case" — she flipped the folder in front of her closed — "I'm ready." Behind David she saw Karen grinning knowingly at her and tilting her head toward David. Karen made the sign for *sexy*, grinned again, and went back to work.

Taming her own grin, Laura went to Beth's office, poked her head in, and announced that she was leaving. Beth said something, with a candy bar in her mouth, not looking up from her desk.

"Tell your stomach to stop growling so I can

hear what you're saying," Laura teased her and Beth looked up guiltily.

"Sorry. It's this damn diet."

"Sounds like a pretty fun diet if it consists of Hershey bars," Laura said.

"That's the problem," Beth moaned. "It doesn't. And I was so strong when I walked past the snack machine. And then that darn Katrina was getting a can of tomato juice out of it and she hit the wrong button . . ."

"So you volunteered to dispose of the Hershey bar for her," Laura finished, laughing.

"That's about the size of it. And the size of *this*" — she half rose and indicated her posterior — "is getting to be extra large."

"Come over one night for dinner," Laura told her, laughing, "and I'll make you a low-cal feast. And you can grumble about your diet all you want."

"It's a deal," Beth said, sighing. "You go ahead and leave. I can see you have someone tall, dark, and handsome waiting for you."

"All right. See you tomorrow."

David drove them to the cabin, where he threw together a casserole from the tiny refrigerator, and a salad. Two bottles of beer completed the meal. "You're getting to be quite the cook," Laura praised him as she tasted the casserole. "Are these water chestnuts in here?"

"I have no idea," he admitted. "I asked Grendel to fix it for me. She made us a cherry pie, too."

"Better make it a small piece for me," Laura said. "I'd feel guilty after all the angst a candy bar caused Beth."

"When we're done," David said, giving her a sideways glance, "I want to show you something."

"What?" she asked, sensing the importance of whatever it was.

"When you're done," David reiterated. He wouldn't answer any more questions, just kept giving her little smiles, so she finished quickly and helped him clear the dishes.

"All right," she said. "What's going on?"

"Come over here and sit down," he insisted, heading for the beat-up couch and patting the cushion beside him.

Suspicious, Laura walked slowly to the couch and sat down. "Okay. Now what?"

"Now read this." He reached behind the couch and pulled out the current copy of Bob Randall's newspaper, the *Courier*. "Bob called me this morning and said he was so impressed with you that he stayed up all night writing this article. He put it in today's paper."

Laura stared at the paper, open to page four, and finally touched it with trembling fingers. She glanced into David's face.

"Read it," he assured her.

She sat stiffly at first as she read, but then she began to relax. It was a good article, and it was complimentary. Bob had recapped the whole mess with the Fielding School for the Deaf and then profiled Buddy Fielding and Laura. She realized that Bob Randall had seen her for what she had been at the time, young, inexperienced, a little too innocent — a victim. He mentioned that she was working as a photographer now, volunteering at the Hastings Institute as well, and he also mentioned that she was seeing David. He ended the piece by calling her a woman of remarkable courage and commitment.

Laura slowly laid the paper on her lap when she finished and took a deep breath before she looked at David.

"Well?" he said.

"I'm sort of numb. I didn't really ever expect to see something nice about myself in print."

"My phone's been ringing all morning," he told her. "Word got around about the article, but no one knew how to find you. I told them you weren't interested in any more interviews. Was that okay? I mean, I have their names if you're interested."

"No," she said quickly, laughing and shaking her head. "I don't want to do any more interviews." Then she sobered and looked at him anxiously. "What did they say about your campaign?"

"You're not a liability, Laura," he said swiftly. "Don't ever imagine that." He shrugged lightly. "They wanted to know how serious our relationship is."

Laura felt her heart leap pounding to her throat. *And what did you tell them?* Only she didn't ask, and he didn't seem inclined to answer at the moment.

"Let's get our coats," he said evasively. "I want to show you something." He gave her a crooked smile. "It's my turn to show you around my home turf."

His home turf was a short car ride away, and she was surprised to find that he had grown up in the country. He had always impressed her as street savvy. He pulled the car onto a gravel road and went about a mile before he stopped in front of a dirt driveway with a deserted farmhouse at the crest of a hill. The house had seen better days, probably years before, and now it was sliding into decay rapidly.

"This was where my parents started out," David said, turning sideways so Laura would be able to read his lips. "Dad grew up on a farm and he bought this property when he and Mom married. They grew corn and soybeans and raised some hogs. They didn't make much money, but they managed to put some aside as the children were born — for a college education."

"They don't sound like people who would divorce," she said, puzzled by this facet of his family background.

He lifted one arm and rested it on the back of the seat. "On the surface, no. But people have hidden sides that others sometimes don't see. Dad was a happy man. He loved the farm and his life. Mom — well, she was someone who had never had much as a child, and when she grew up I guess she felt she'd earned the right to expect more from life. Nothing was ever quite right for her, not good enough, not perfect enough. She loved us kids, but we never quite measured up either."

"What happened when they divorced?"

"Erin was only two. Mom had custody of her and Dad got custody of the rest of the kids. That was unusual in those days, but Mom had suggested it herself. I think she'd felt cheated out of her own childhood, and I suppose deep down she knew that Dad would give us all a better childhood than she could." He stared out the window at the bare trees shivering in the wind and said, "A year later Erin came to live with the rest of us. Mom and Dad both remarried, but Dad's new wife didn't care much for the farm, so she ran her own store in town, and Grendel came to take care of us kids."

"Erin told me you were the one who kept the kids together." She watched his face, saw old pain, bittersweet memories, a trace of sadness.

"I think I saw it as my appointed duty," he said dryly. "I tried to be the other parent in the family." He looked into her face and smiled mirthlessly. "One time when Erin was four and I was telling her to retie her sneakers she told me to lay off, that I was never going to replace Mom, and I — laid off. We were a close bunch of kids anyway, so what fighting we did was the innocent kind. And Grendel was a stabilizing force in our lives. We've stayed close over the years. When

Dad died, Alan tried to run the farm, but it was a losing proposition, so we had to sell it. No one lives in the house now. A neighboring farmer bought it and works the land."

His fingers brushed the nape of her neck and she felt that familiar awareness of him as a lover, the quickening response of her pulse and the need that rose in her like physical hunger. He stroked her softly, watching her face. "I don't take happiness for granted, Laura," he said carefully. "I saw how my mother couldn't find it and how my father lost it, and I knew I was lucky to have it in my own marriage."

Her breath caught, and her heart pounded erratically. *His marriage.* Her own mental image of Barbara flashed through her mind — a warm, laughing artistic woman who presided over her family lovingly. And juxtaposed beside that image was the picture of Buddy telling Laura she just didn't measure up.

She opened her mouth, knowing deep inside what he was going to say, wanting to keep him from saying it for some dark reason she didn't understand, but his finger moved gently to touch her lips and stop the words.

"Marry me, Laura," he said, staring into her face. When she didn't answer his mouth tightened. "Don't run away now," he implored her, his finger tracing soft patterns over her lips. "I can see that panic in your eyes, honey, and I know why it's there. But we can make it work. I know we can. I love you."

I love you, she cried inside. *But I don't know if I can marry you.* "I don't know," she said honestly, feeling the words vibrate against his finger.

"You're scared?" he asked, lowering his hand to cup her jaw. "Of what? Me? The life of a politician's wife? Hell, I'll drop out of the race. It's not the sole purpose of my life."

She shook her head quickly. "No! I won't let you change your whole life for me. And I'm not afraid of you. Just of coping — of *not* coping."

"I know it's difficult," he said after a while. "And I know I'm asking a lot of you to take on two children, a politician's wife's hectic schedule. But I'm selfish enough to ask you to do it, Laura, because I need you in my life. I need you badly." She could see the truth of his words in the crystal-clear blue eyes watching her, along with a trace of impatience at her hesitation.

"David," she said helplessly, pleading with her eyes. "What am I supposed to say? That of course we can overcome every obstacle? That it would be a piece of cake? We're both too old to buy that kind of fantasy."

"And we're both too old to shy away from a commitment just because it might get tough," he insisted, the tension around his mouth deepening. "Listen to yourself, Laura — listen to what you're saying! That just because we know what we're getting into it's doomed! There aren't any gilt-edged guarantees in life, but when you find someone you love you have to take a chance." His eyes, darkening to gray, searched hers relentlessly and both hands gripped her shoulders. "Do you love me, Laura?"

"Yes!" She closed her eyes briefly, then opened them. "Yes. And I don't want to hurt you."

He released her and ran one weary hand over his eyes. "We're hurting each other now, Laura. We belong together. You're the best part of my life and I — I think I'm good for you."

He leaned back in the seat and looked into her face, and she had to look away from the sadness she saw there. It would work, her inner voice of reason told her. She was realistic enough to know it wouldn't be easy, but she and David were survivors. They didn't let life slip through their fingers. They fought for what they wanted. And she wanted David . . .

Slowly she placed one hand over his on the seat. "David," she said shakily. "Just give me some time to do some thinking. Okay?"

"Hell, honey," he said, his eyes still sad. "One thing I've learned is that time is in short supply in life. Don't take too long."

"Oh, David," she said, hating the way she was hurting them both, but he silenced her with a hungry kiss.

"Have you had any problems?" Dr. Sarnoff asked Laura when she was seated in his examining room and he was reviewing her chart.

"Some minor ones," she said, holding her hands rigidly still in her lap. "My hearing aid

206

doesn't seem to be picking up sounds as well as it did."

He frowned, but quickly glanced up at Laura with a smile. "Well, we'll check everything out. Let's do the audiometry tests first." He led her down the hall to the small booth that had become so familiar to her in her childhood. Dr. Sarnoff's nurse, Sue, who had been with him for fifteen years, adjusted the headset over Laura's ears and gave her an encouraging smile. *Just relax,* she mouthed, *and raise your hand each time you hear a tone.*

Laura nodded and tried to return the smile, used to the routine. She made the hand sign for *pretty* and pointed to Sue's new hairdo. Sue grinned and made the sign for *expensive.*

Then the testing began in earnest and Laura lost track of time as she concentrated on the silence, waiting for the sounds. To stem her rising nervousness she closed her eyes and summoned up David's face as he'd proposed to her yesterday.

Laura was sitting on the couch, absently stroking Horton's ears, when he suddenly glanced at the door and began barking and pawing her leg. Laura looked and saw the light for the doorbell was on. "Good boy," she praised Horton and got up wearily.

Beth was sagging against the door wearing a look of utter starvation and weakness and she made a brave attempt to sniff the air. "Don't tell me," she moaned. "Salad."

Laura couldn't think for a moment and then she clapped a hand to her forehead. "Oh, Beth, I'm sorry! I forgot all about our dinner!"

"Leave it to a thin person to forget a meal," Beth observed, walking into the apartment, and then she frowned over her shoulder. "Laura, what's wrong? You look like you just lost your best friend. Really, it doesn't matter about dinner. We'll order out for pizza. It's got lots of protein, and tomato sauce is practically a vegetable." She turned around and studied her friend. "Laura?" she continued, her humorous expression fleeing. "What's wrong?"

Laura could feel her mouth trembling. "I went to the doctor today."

"Sit down here," Beth ordered, leading Laura to the couch and taking the seat next to her. "What did he say?"

Laura made a feeble attempt to smile wryly. "The official verdict is 'a loss of residual hearing.' "

"And what's the translation?" Beth demanded.

"He said the nerve has degenerated — it happened in the other ear when I was in high school — and they told me then it could happen again." Her chest hurt from her raspy breathing. "Dr. Sarnoff says I've been compensating by lipreading and I didn't realize my hearing had deteriorated to such a degree." She raised stricken eyes to her friend's face. "Beth, I'm profoundly deaf."

"Oh, my God," Beth whispered, stunned. Her eyes went to Laura's ear. "I didn't even realize you weren't wearing your aid."

This time Laura did manage a wry twist of her lips. "It seemed pretty useless as jewelry," she said.

"Oh, you poor kid," Beth commiserated, putting her arm around Laura's shoulders. And that's when Laura let herself go and did what she hadn't been able to do since she got home — cry.

It seemed ages later that the tears stopped, and Laura raised her face, drained. "I'm sorry," she said hoarsely, her voice still trembling. "I didn't mean to dump all over you. Dr. Sarnoff gave me the name of the leader of a local support group. He said it would be an emotional adjustment for me, and I guess he was right."

"Laura Kincaid, don't you ever worry about dumping on me!" Beth began, but Laura held up her hand.

"Let me dry my eyes," she said, "so I can see your lips." She came back to the couch with a tissue and wiped both eyes, then smiled at Beth. "Okay, coach, give me your pep talk."

"First," Beth said, "we've been friends too long for you to worry about dumping on me. Second, you're the strongest person I know, and this is only the second time I've ever seen you cry. You're going to deal with this. I know you. And the support group sounds like a good idea." She held up her hand. "And third — I'm starved. How about that pizza?"

Laura laughed for the first time since she'd left the doctor's office. "All right, but you have to call. And don't get anchovies." She watched as Beth picked up the phone and moved aside the CODE-COM set. There was an identical set at the Hastings Institute, and when Anne called Laura she sent her message in coded light flashes that showed on the dark rectangle in the top of the set. "Beth," Laura said in distraction, the Hastings Institute bringing back other memories. "David asked me to marry him."

Laura's announcement had the same effect on Beth as if she'd just won the lottery. Beth dropped the phone and ran back to Laura, standing in front of her and trying to see her face. "That's wonderful! What did you tell him?" Laura looked away, and Beth tapped her shoulder. "You said yes, didn't you?"

"I told him I had to think about it."

"Come on, Laura! That's what you say when someone offers you jalapeño peppers for the first time! This is marriage! And to a great guy who loves you."

"And why are you so sure he loves me?" Laura asked.

Beth hiked her hands on her hips. "Because you don't have to read lips to see it all over his face. He's crazy about you, Laura!"

"Beth, I can't marry him. Not now."

"And why not? Because you're deaf? Honey, I don't know what difference that makes. I'm sure David doesn't give a damn."

210

"That's just it. It doesn't matter to David now, but he's got a career and two children, and I don't want to be a burden on anyone."

She looked away, and Beth touched her shoulder to get her attention. "It's Buddy, isn't it?" Beth said. "Remember? One time you told me the things he said to you."

"Yeah," Laura admitted wryly. "One vodka martini and I spilled my guts to you."

"Look," Beth said. "I'm no help to you when my stomach is about to lead an armed revolt against me, so I'm going to order that pizza. Then we'll talk."

Beth sank down onto the couch after she'd ordered and studied Laura's face. "What are you going to tell David?" she asked.

"I don't know," Laura said wearily. She shook her head. "I just don't know."

The doorbell rang later that night, after Beth had gone. Laura saw the light and shushed Horton, who was bouncing up and down in front of her and barking. She stroked his head to quiet him and gave him a treat, but she didn't answer the door. She was pretty sure she knew who it was and she wasn't ready to face him yet.

She stood at the window of her bedroom that night, feeling almost entombed in the darkness and silence. A streetlight burned faintly below and a couple strolled leisurely down the sidewalk. They stopped just inside the pool of light and although she couldn't read their lips from such a distance, Laura could see that they were laughing and enjoying each other's company. The man put his arm around the woman and bent to kiss her teasingly, a brief peck on the cheek. His companion pretended to be annoyed, but she was smiling. And then he really kissed her and Laura thought her heart would break watching them. She went back to bed and pulled the quilt all the way to her nose, as if she could hide from the rest of the world.

Everything was falling through her grasp. She tried to rationalize marrying David, but in all honesty she couldn't see the way. He needed someone with all five senses intact, who could aid *him,* not someone who needed assistance with the phone or in communicating with strangers. Someone . . . who would hear the love words he spoke in bed.

The next afternoon, after work, Laura took a bus to the Hastings Institute. Beth had been so-licitous all day and had even suggested a further breach of her diet, inviting Laura to go have a drink and a long lunch, but Laura said she had a lot of work to catch up. It was partially true — she'd been putting off looking over the pictures she had taken of David's house.

She was lost in thought on the bus but soon became aware of the heavyset woman in the win-dow seat next to her who was now standing up in agitation. Laura looked over at her just in time to read her lips. "God almighty, lady! I said my stop's coming up and I gotta get out. Are you deaf and dumb?"

Laura swung her legs aside for the woman and eyed her coolly. "As a matter of fact, yes, I am deaf. And no, I'm not dumb." Usually she didn't respond when someone made a remark like that, but her patience was thin today. The woman's face turned a bright crimson as she edged past.

A breathless Anne caught up with Laura in the hall as Laura was heading toward Clara's class. "Whew!" Anne cried when Laura turned at the touch on her shoulder. "I've been chasing you for two minutes. Turn up your volume. I hollered and hollered."

Laura smiled apologetically and gave a wry shrug. "Sorry. There's been a problem."

Anne glanced at Laura's ear, unadorned, and frowned. "What's wrong?"

"It's been gradual and I didn't notice, but I've lost my residual hearing — not that there was much to lose anyway."

"Oh, I'm so sorry," Anne said, worried eyes searching Laura's face. "Is there anything I can do?"

"As a matter of fact, yes. I've been thinking about that offer of the assistant directorship here — and I think I'd like a shot at it. I'm going by the college tomorrow to look into classes and see what we can work out as far as my keeping up with the lectures."

"That's wonderful," Anne said, the worry changing to relief. "I'll talk with the admissions

213

department if you'd like. I'm sure they can arrange for you to get a transcript of the class lectures."

"That's what I'm hoping. Thanks, Anne. And, Anne — I'd appreciate it if you didn't tell anyone else yet about my hearing loss. I think I need a little time to adjust."

"Sure. I understand." Anne gave her a reassuring pat on the shoulder. "What I was chasing you for was along the same lines. The phone has rung off the hook ever since that article appeared about you. They all want interviews." She gave Laura a helpless shrug.

Laura smiled. "Well, tell them I'll contact them later — after I get going on college."

"Okay. See you later."

Julie came out of a classroom and nearly collided with Laura. "Boy, am I glad to see you!" Julie said in relief. "Clara needs some individual work and I'm swamped today. Can you do it?"

"Sure. Where is she?"

"I just put her in room five. I was about to recruit Anne for the job."

"No problem. How's her attention span today?"

"Not bad. I think she'll sit still a while for you."

Laura went to room five and peered in the door. Clara was busily fitting colored shapes into a puzzle board on the table. Laura bent down to pound her fists on a nearby chair and then smiled and waved when Clara looked around.

"Hi, Clara," she said loudly and clearly.

"Haaaaa," Clara answered, grinning at the sight of Laura.

"Good girl!" Laura praised her, lowering herself to sit cross-legged on the floor beside the girl and tucking her skirt around her knees. "Clara's talking."

Clara grinned again and pointed to a book on the table. "Bu — bu," she said.

"Do you want to hear a story?" Laura said, and Clara nodded vigorously.

So Laura began telling Clara a story, opening the book so the little girl could see the pictures. She stopped frequently to ask Clara a question about the story or to ask her what a particular picture was, and she was happy with the progress Clara had made. She was making basic sounds now and, most importantly, she was learning to communicate.

Half an hour into the story, Laura could see Clara's attention waning, so she wrapped up the story and let Clara wander off to a corner where the dolls were. Laura watched her a minute as she held a doll close to her chest and rocked it, her eyes closed, and then she sensed someone else in the room.

She turned around and saw David standing in the doorway, Mary and Jean with him. Laura clambered to her feet, feeling as though her heart hadn't quite made it off the floor with her.

"Hi! What are you doing?" Mary said, striding into the room in her imperious style.

"Anne told us you were in here," David said, his eyes probing Laura's face. "Is it all right if we watch?"

Laura was working hard to catch everything Mary and David had said, glancing from face to face so she wouldn't miss anything. "Of course," Laura said. "Come on in." She moved toward them and smiled at the girls. "Clara's playing in the corner if you want to join her. She's just learning to talk."

"Is she deaf?" Jean asked.

"Yes, honey," Laura said, feeling an ache inside as she said the word. Jean joined Mary and Clara in the corner.

Laura turned back to David in time to catch him saying, "I came by your place last night." There was a hesitancy on his face that hadn't been there before, and she knew it was because of her.

"I must have been asleep," she lied. "Horton tried to get me up once, but I told him to go away." She gave what she hoped was an apologetic smile.

David nodded slowly, but she could see the wariness in his eyes. "Laura, we have to talk," he said.

"I'm kind of busy now," she hedged.

"What's wrong?" he demanded. "Something's wrong, isn't it?" When she didn't answer, he said, "Dammit, Laura, talk to me. We've at least been honest with each other."

"It's nothing," she said, hoping her voice

wasn't loud enough for the children to hear. "I'm tired, and I've got a lot to do."

He was silent for a minute, studying her face, but she wouldn't look into his eyes. "This is it, isn't it?" he said finally, and she had to piece together the words because his mouth was tight. "You're trying to tell me it's over, aren't you?" She still couldn't find anything to say that would make this any easier and he said, "At least have the guts to tell me to my face, Laura."

Laura glanced over her shoulder at the children and then back at David. Apparently interpreting her hesitancy as worry about fighting in front of them, he motioned her into the hall. She didn't want to go, didn't want to have to tell him what she knew she would, but she went.

"Laura, I love you, and I think you love me," he said when they were alone. "Whatever it is, we can work it out."

"David, our lives just won't work together," she said, trying to make him understand. "I'm going back to school and I'm going to accept the job of assistant director here. When Anne leaves, in all probability I'll become director."

"So? Laura, I'm *glad* you're going to school. I'm *glad* you're going to be the director. I want you to be everything you want to be. But, hell, honey, I don't see anything in that that means we can't get married."

"I just don't think I'm ready to get married," she said, finally letting her eyes meet his and feeling a sudden need to lean against the wall.

"You're not —" he began and then his eyes swung quickly to the room behind them. David looked back at Laura, who was still watching him, and frowned. "You didn't hear that, did you?" he said slowly, his eyes searching her face.

Quickly she glanced behind her and saw that the classroom door had blown shut. It would have been a pretty loud noise, she realized. She looked back at David. "Loud noises don't bother me."

His eyes had moved to her ear, and he was still frowning. "You're not wearing your hearing aid. Laura?"

She looked away and managed to swing her eyes back to his face again. "No, I'm not."

He moved to put his hands on her shoulders, but she flinched and he brought them to rest on the wall on either side of her instead. He bent down to see her face. "You went to the doctor?" His eyes were anxious, cloudy. "What did he say?"

"He said I don't have to wear the hearing aid anymore," she said dryly. Then: "I'm sorry. I didn't mean to be flippant." She clipped the words out. "I've lost all residual hearing. I'm deaf." To emphasize her point, she spelled out the word in sign language, a letter at a time.

David's hand closed over hers, trapping it in mid-letter. "God, Laura! I'm sorry. I know how hard this is for you —"

"No!" she cried, interrupting him. "Don't say it doesn't matter! I don't think I can stand to have one more person tell a deaf person that they'll adjust! 'You'll do fine,' they say. 'You'll be able to speak well enough to make yourself understood. You'll be able to rejoin *"normal"* society.' Well, I'm not 'normal,' David, and neither are the kids in this school! We can't hear and sometimes people aren't very nice to us. And still I have to push these kids and assure them that what we're making them do is all for the best. Well, some things aren't for the best, and, David, our being together is one of those things."

"Laura," he began helplessly, and the pain in his eyes nearly overwhelmed her. "You're acting like marriage is some terrible thing I'm trying to force on you just because hearing people do it! That's not true and you know it. I want to marry you because I need you in my life!"

"You don't know!" she said. "Do you need someone in your life who has the whole house wired with lights to compensate for the sounds she can't hear? Do you need a wife whose speech will deteriorate over time because she can't hear herself any longer? Picture that, David! A press conference. The reporters ask your wife how she feels about something or other and she answers, only her words are slurred, unclear, difficult to understand. And there it is, all captured on film for posterity." She realized she'd hit him hard when he looked away before he'd meet her eyes again. She made herself speak calmly. "A lot of people hear deaf people speak and assume they're intellectually deficient. *Deaf and dumb.* That's what people say. And what they mean is deaf and stupid. Do you really want that, David?"

His eyes were burning when he spoke, and even if she couldn't hear the words she could see the intensity on his face in the taut lines around his eyes and mouth. "I want you! I don't give a damn about the rest! If you don't want to go through the public crap with me then that's fine. But if you want to go and try to change people's perceptions of the deaf — then that's fine too! All I know is that my life was empty before I met you and now I give a damn about things again. Most of all, I give a damn about you." His hands slipped to her shoulders and this time she didn't move. "I don't think it's the fact that I'm in the public eye that's bothering you, Laura. I don't even think you seriously believe your deafness is too big a challenge for us. I think you're scared, Laura — scared to death that what we have would slowly wither and die like your marriage to Buddy did. You're scared of failing. So you're going to cut us off before we ever have to meet some of those tough obstacles waiting out there."

"It's not like that, David!" Oh, Lord! She wanted him so and she just couldn't see a way through this thicket of problems.

"Isn't it?" His thumbs had begun a slow massage of her collarbones, almost against their will, and now he removed his hands with effort. "We could work it out, Laura. I know that, and I think somewhere deep down you know it, too. It might not be easy and it wouldn't always be smooth sailing, but we could do it. I can't make you do it all by myself, Laura. You have to want it, too. I'll always be there to help if you need me." Her heart twisted at the anguish in his eyes. "And now, I'm going to take the girls home before I start crying right here in the middle of the school." With that, he turned away and Laura saw him call to the girls from the doorway. Their faces were anxious and scared when they came out, and Laura tried to smile for them, but it felt like a parody of a smile locked on her mouth.

"I'll see you later," she said to them. "Thanks for coming."

"Will you really see us later?" Mary turned around to ask as David began herding them away.

Laura's throat constricted. Would she? "I hope so," she said, but it felt more like a question.

When the girls were again walking up the hall, David turned around and stopped briefly. If her heart needed one more act to break it in two it was when he looked at her solemnly, pointed to himself, crossed his wrists over his chest, and then pointed to her. *I love you.*

Chapter 10

"So how are classes going?" Anne asked Laura and Karen as she leaned back in her chair and repositioned a pin holding the twist of hair at her neck in place.

"Pretty well," Laura said. She glanced at Karen, and Karen nodded enthusiastically. *The student lounge is fantastic!* Karen signed, and Laura laughed.

When Karen found out that Laura was taking classes toward her degree, she had asked about enrolling too, and the two had bolstered each other through the last three weeks. They had enrolled late, but since they had to have transcripts of the lectures anyway, their instructors let them catch up.

"You know, we've gotten a lot of calls about your appointment as assistant director, Laura," Anne said. "Don't look so worried," she rushed to assure her. "They were all very supportive. A lot of people saw you on the news last night explaining how much we need a large van to transport kids on field trips." Anne reached into her drawer and pulled out a handful of checks. "These came in the mail today," she said, smiling. "Over ten thousand dollars' worth. And" —

she held up one check and pretended to scrutinize it before she handed it to Laura — "this one for one thousand dollars alone."

Laura's pulse grew thready as she saw the signature on the check. *David Evers.* She looked up at Anne quickly.

Anne must have known what she was thinking because she said, "No, there was no note with it."

Karen tapped Laura's arm and signed, *Don't worry. He's just giving you time.*

"I'm not so sure," Laura said distractedly. She hadn't realized how much she would miss David, and this kind of pain was a revelation to her. She had felt an aching emptiness at other times in her life, but it was always for something wishful, like an easier life without the struggle to compensate for her lack of hearing. And it always passed in a day or two as she made herself get going with her life. But the ache she'd felt since David was gone was so ferocious that she could feel it clamoring inside her night and day, wanting only one thing to relieve the emptiness — David. College and the assistant directorship hadn't alleviated it one iota. If anything, she needed him more than ever to balance her universe.

Laura saw a movement at the door from the corner of her eye and glanced over. She stood up in surprise when she saw Mary and Jean, and couldn't stop herself from looking hopefully over their shoulders. But David wasn't with them.

They looked unsure of their welcome, and Laura hurried to them, hugging them fiercely and pulling them inside the room. They nodded and smiled when she introduced them to Anne and Karen, and Laura was touched to see them sign *hi* back to Karen.

"What are you doing here?" she asked, pulling up two chairs for them and sitting directly in front of them so she could read their lips.

Mary looked at Jean and took the lead. "We want to help out here."

"You mean work with the kids?" Laura said hesitantly.

Mary nodded. "If we could. I'm working on a Girl Scout badge, and Jean said she wanted to help me." Mary apparently wanted to say something else, but didn't.

"Dad wouldn't let us come at first," Jean said, "but we talked him into it."

Mary gave her a sideways kick and Jean said, "Ow," and looked offended. "Well it's true!" Jean said indignantly.

"How did you get here?" Laura asked.

"We took the bus," Mary said, still throwing irritated looks at Jean.

"So you want to help with the kids," Laura said, and both girls nodded an eager yes. Laura wasn't at all sure of their motives, and she looked at Anne questioningly. It wouldn't help anybody for the girls to let some of the children grow attached to them and then quit. But Anne didn't seem worried and gave Laura a movement of the head that said *why not?*

"All right," Laura said. "Let's go find Julie and she can get you started."

Laura voted in the primary in March, and that night she watched the returns on TV. The local news wasn't close-captioned, so she had to follow the totals as they were flashed on the screen. When David won handily, Laura felt a large measure of triumph on his behalf and an even larger measure of loss because she couldn't share his victory with him.

The girls were still showing up regularly at the institute and they seemed to enjoy the time they spent with the children, playing games or reading them stories. And Jean had developed a rapport with Clara to the extent that Clara adored Jean and wouldn't let her out of her sight.

Still, Laura felt as though a door was locked somewhere and that she would be frozen in time until the key turned in the lock. She didn't fully understand the feeling, just knew that it had to do with her and David and the reasons they weren't together. So for now, as March blustered toward spring, Laura tried to ride out the turmoil inside her heart.

Then came the crisis with Clara. She had made remarkable progress until her mother decided to try to become reconciled with Clara's father. And Clara was caught in the middle as her father moved back to the house, the father she didn't remember.

"She's angry," Julie told Laura as they walked down the hall. Laura had come to the institute straight from her afternoon classes. She was working only mornings at *Springfield Today* now. "She screams when anyone comes near her," Julie said. "We've had to take her out of her class with the other children for now. And she's had to quit going to the hearing nursery school those three afternoons a week."

"What about her parents?" Laura asked. "What do they think?"

"Who knows?" Julie said meaningfully. "Right now what Clara's mother wants is Clara's father, and apparently what he wants is to reconcile only if he can maintain his free-and-easy lifestyle. And they're both using Clara as a pawn. You know, the mother says, 'Your poor little daughter needs a father,' and he says, 'I'd be glad to be her father if you'd just loosen up a bit.'"

"And so Clara thinks that if this doesn't work out it's her fault," Laura finished.

"You got it," Julie said.

"Poor kid."

"Yeah. Jean's with her now. At least Clara wasn't screaming when I left."

Clara was sitting sullenly in the corner clutching a doll and Jean was sitting cross-legged on the floor near her reading from a book when Julie and Laura entered the room. Clara was obviously torn between wanting the book and wanting to maintain her anger and stubborn-

226

ness. So she was staring out the window and throwing furtive, dark glances Jean's way.

"Hi, honey," Laura said to Jean, briefly touching her hair.

"Hi, Laura," Jean said warmly, her eyes lighting up at the sight of Laura. "Clara's quiet now, but she's still mad."

"Hi there, Clara!" Laura said brightly, squatting down beside the little girl. "So you're mad today, are you? Can you say *temper tantrum?* T-t-t-t. Can you make that sound, Clara?"

Clara crossed her arms stubbornly and glared out the window at the world in general.

"Well, I don't blame you," Laura said. "Sometimes you just have to get mad. Did you ever hear about the little chicken that got mad because the sun wouldn't shine?" She saw Clara's resolution waver for a fraction of a second as her eyes darted to Laura and then away again, and Laura glanced over her shoulder at Julie. Julie made the *okay* sign and backed out of the room.

Laura made up the story on the spur of the moment, pretending to tell it to Jean instead of Clara. From the corner of her eye she tried to gauge Clara's mood as she elaborated the little chicken's problems on one of those days when nothing seemed to go right. First the sun wouldn't shine and then it rained and got the little chicken's breakfast wet and then a bigger, older, more experienced rooster came to the barnyard and started romancing the little chicken's mama. It was obvious that Clara was paying attention now and watching Laura's face and hands, eager to get all of the story. Laura prodded her brain cells to come up with a happy ending to the little chicken's dilemma, to let Clara know it was all right to be angry but that there were ways of working out that anger.

Laura was so caught up in inventing a proper end to the story that she didn't realize that Clara's attention was diverted until she saw her stand up suddenly. Jean was looking toward the door, and Laura turned around too. Anne was trying to calm a woman who, from the strong resemblance, Laura guessed to be Clara's mother. Laura read Anne's lips and realized she was trying to get the woman to leave until she relaxed.

"But I want her home with me!" the mother, near tears, was saying. "If her father doesn't want her with us it doesn't matter, because I do!"

"Please, Mrs. Sanders," Anne pleaded. "You're not doing the child any good like this. It won't help anyone to just take her out of school."

"But I'm all alone," the woman said, crying now. "Her father says he can't handle a deaf child. He's gone away again."

"I'm sorry," Anne said soothingly. "Let's go to my office and talk until you feel better." Anne was trying to maneuver Mrs. Sanders out of the room, and Laura instinctively looked at Clara.

The little girl was standing stonily, pure fury on her face.

Anne almost had her out in the hall when Mrs. Sanders turned back and called Clara's name. She knelt down and held out her arms. "Come to Mother, baby!" she called, tears on her face.

Clara opened her mouth and a furious, helpless wail of sound came out. The doll she was holding hit the floor and she ran away from her mother, looking over her shoulder in defiance.

Laura scrambled to her feet when she saw the tiny girl headed straight for the stereo resting on a metal file cabinet. The teachers sometimes put a record on the stereo and turned it up full blast to let the children feel the beat through their hands or feet. It seemed to help them with speech rhythm. But Clara wasn't looking at where she was going and Laura knew she was going to crash into the file cabinet.

Jean was even faster than Laura and reached the child a split second before Laura did. Even so, it was a split second too late as Clara ran full tilt into the cabinet.

Everything seemed to happen in slow motion. The stereo slid to the edge of the cabinet and both Jean and Laura lunged for it. Clara fell down right in front of Laura, and Laura tripped over her and went sprawling on the floor. She could only watch in horror as Jean and the stereo both went crashing to the floor in front of her. Laura could feel the thud reverberate through the floor.

Anne and Mrs. Sanders were there in the next instant, bending over Clara, who was crying with her mouth wide open and her eyes screwed shut. Laura scrambled up and rushed to Jean, who still lay on the floor, what was left of the stereo more or less on top of her. Laura jerked the stereo off the girl and pitched it onto the floor, hastily brushing away pieces of broken plastic from the cover. She knelt down beside Jean and made an anxious visual inspection. The only injury seemed to be a deep cut on her forearm. Jean took one glance at the cut, turned ashen, and looked at Laura.

"It's all right, honey," Laura soothed her. "Everything's going to be fine. Just lie still and hold your arm up high. That's a girl."

She pulled the scarf from around her neck and tied it over the cut, pressing her fingers gently to stop the flow of blood. She gave Jean a reassuring smile and said, "I guess even the little chicken didn't have this much excitement in one day." Jean gave her the reaction she'd hoped for and smiled back.

Anne came to kneel on the other side of Jean, speaking so Laura could see her face. "Clara seems to be okay. I think she's just frightened. I'm going with Mrs. Sanders in her car to Clara's pediatrician. I'll tell Julie to drive you and Jean to the hospital." Laura nodded, and Anne gave Jean a light squeeze on the shoulder.

Laura sat in the hospital corridor, one anxious

face among a sea of anxious faces shifting restlessly on hard-backed chairs, waiting for the doctor to finish treating Jean. Julie touched her arm, and when Laura looked up she said, "Here, I brought you some coffee."

"Thanks, Julie. It always seems to take forever in hospitals, doesn't it?" Julie nodded and sat down beside Laura.

Laura had given the doctor all the necessary information and filled out the insurance forms for the hospital, and it was Julie who had called David's house. She'd told Laura an older woman had answered, so Laura assumed it was Grendel who would come to the hospital to pick up Jean.

She looked down the hall and saw Anne walking toward them. Handing Julie her coffee, she went to meet her. "How's Clara?" she asked immediately, searching Anne's face.

"Just fine. She was only shaken up. I think it got rid of some of her anger to have her mother be the one to comfort her after the accident. How's Jean?"

"Fine, as far as I know. The doctor wouldn't let me stay while he did the stitches. Julie called her family."

Anne laid her hand on Laura's arm. "Laura, I know you've had some qualms in the past about taking on the job of assistant director, but you handled everything beautifully today. In fact, you've been doing an excellent job in all areas. I can't thank you enough. I may even retire early."

231

"Don't you dare!" Laura warned her, but she was smiling. It was true: She wasn't the same woman who'd been married to Buddy Fielding, the young girl who was too insecure and unsure of herself to question anything Buddy did, much less his unkind assessment of her as a woman and a lover. She had grown strong and capable and she knew how to take hold of life with both hands. So why wasn't she with David? her heart insisted. Good question, she admitted. In fact, it was a damn good question. "Excuse me a minute, Anne," she said, sobering when she saw Grendel hurrying down the hall, her eyes anxiously scanning the faces.

Grendel's eyes brightened when she saw Laura. "How is she?" she asked immediately.

"She's fine," Laura assured her. "The doctor told me the cut wasn't bad. He wanted to clean it and put in five or six stitches. She's right in there." She indicated the door, and Grendel started for it, then stopped.

"Laura," she said, turning around, and Laura saw the worry in her face. "David misses you. We all do, but . . . I think it's different with him. He's become a very sad man lately."

"I miss him, too," Laura said.

Grendel studied Laura's face a moment. "I know where he'll be tonight," she said meaningfully. "He has to write a speech."

Laura stopped her car behind David's truck at the cabin and turned off the engine. She sat

232

there a minute in the darkness and then resolutely got out. She looked around at the trees unfurling tiny buds of leaves and felt the soft wind on her skin. She tried to think of the sounds she associated with spring and smiled when they came to her in memory, although dim and distorted with time. The squeaky-gate chirp of birds, children's roller skates rumbling over sidewalks, the frisky yapping of dogs feeling young again because it was spring. She wouldn't hear those things again, but she really didn't mind, because there were so many other things she heard in her heart.

Her breath caught when she saw him down by the pond, a straight, lean, lonely figure, his hands in his pockets. He was staring out over the pond at a faint remnant of the sunset, the sky glowing like the blush on a peach. She wanted to run to him, but he hadn't heard the car and hadn't turned around, and suddenly she was shy.

She picked her way toward him over rough ground stippled with new shoots of grass and dandelions. She stopped and said his name hesitantly when she was only ten feet away, and he turned sharply.

Memory must have failed her whenever she had summoned up his image these last few days — because he was even handsomer here and now. Oh, he was beautiful! And such eyes, now full of heat and pain. Pain she'd caused.

She saw him blank his expression, hide the need from her.

She wondered if her voice was shaking as much as she was. "Is Jean all right?" she asked.

He nodded. "She says you took good care of her. Thank you."

"I'm sorry about the accident." She couldn't hear his voice, but the expression on his face was strained and wary.

"Look, Laura, you didn't have to come out here to offer an apology. Jean's fine, and I know those things happen. She can still come to the institute if she wants."

"David, won't you even talk to me anymore?" she asked helplessly, tears gathering in her throat.

"No, Laura! I'm not good at this. For God's sake, do you think I can stand for us to be just friends now?" He turned away abruptly and strode toward the cabin.

The tears were choking her as she watched him go. "David, I need you." She wasn't even sure she'd actually said it until he stopped and slowly turned around. "This isn't easy for me either," she said, feeling the trembling of her body. "I'm crossing another bridge, but I don't want to do it alone. I want to do it with you. I love you, David."

"Laura." She saw the hesitancy on his face, the way he made her name almost a question, and then the slow dawning of life as the pain began to recede from his eyes. "I've missed you. God, how I've missed you." He took two steps toward her, stopped, and his hands were shaky as he slowly pointed to himself, crossed his wrists over his chest, and . . .

And she was crying by the time he pointed to her. She repeated his signs quickly, her heart full of tears. She loved him so!

When his arms came around her she turned her mouth up to his. Hungry . . . hungry . . . so hungry. *Touch me,* her hands told him. *Love me.*

"Wait, wait," he was telling her when she looked at his mouth. He was smiling crookedly as he caught her hands in his. "I'm not fast yet," he told her. "But I'm learning."

She didn't understand until he began signing, slowly and haltingly. *I want you to share my life. Will you marry me?*

Laura's fingers caught his as he finished. Her answer was to kiss him — long and hard.

Epilogue

"Did you *see* that wedding cake Grendel made?" Beth asked, a dieter's lust in her eyes as she mouthed the question.

Laura laughed. "I know. I told her not to go to any trouble, but she said she wanted to go to trouble and that was that."

"It's got to be three feet tall," Beth breathed. "And the two figures on top — where on earth did she find a bride and groom signing *I love you? Lord*," she moaned. "I'll split the seams on this dress before the reception even gets underway, just from looking at the icing — *that's* how fattening that wedding cake is."

The last of the guests were arriving at the church, and Laura peeked out at them from the small room off the vestibule. It was a beautiful day for a wedding. She'd always wanted to be a December bride, and the day had dawned crisp and clear with a forecast for snow that night.

Grendel came bustling up to them, frowning as she surveyed Beth. "You ate a candy bar at lunch, didn't you?" she accused Beth, whipping out a needle and thread without waiting for an answer and taking several small precise stitches at the side of Beth's pink bridesmaid dress.

"Oh, God," Beth said. "How does the woman know these things? I might as well have Hershey tattooed on my forehead."

Grendel moved over to Laura and hugged her. "Beautiful," she murmured, shaking her head and hugging her hard again.

Satisfied with her last-minute repair, Grendel retreated to the vestibule. An obviously worried minister was the next one to appear in front of Laura. "Miss Kincaid," he shouted, "about that music."

"It's all right, Reverend Martin," Laura told him, seeing the strain on his face and suppressing a smile. "You don't have to shout. I can read your lips."

"Well, Miss Kincaid, I just got another call from the neighbors. They wanted to know if we're holding a rock concert over here."

"It's only for a little longer," she coaxed him. "You see, many of the people here today are deaf and they can't hear music. But they can feel the vibrations through their hands and feet if it's loud enough."

"Oh, my, yes, it's loud enough," he assured her. "Oh, yes. I can't say I've ever heard Mozart played quite that loudly before." He started to leave and then turned back, obviously reluctant to bring up what he was about to say. "Miss Kincaid," he began hesitantly. "There's a large dog in the last pew."

"Which side is he on?" she asked him, trying

to be serious about this.

"The left."

"Well, good. He's more a friend of the bride than the groom."

"Yes, well . . ." Reverend Martin let that trail off and nodded vacantly as he backed out of the room.

Beth looked at Laura and they both started chuckling when he was gone. "I don't think he'll ever recover from this wedding," Laura said.

The vibrations in the floor stopped, and Laura peered out. Reverend Martin was entering the church from a side door, followed by David and Alan. Laura took a deep breath and held it. He was so gorgeous in his tux, his dark hair and blue eyes set off by his black jacket. *State Senator David Evers.* To her surprise, David was the one who had suggested they not get married until the election was over — even though he would probably die of a hormonal overload, he teased her. But he wanted her to be sure. He wanted her to really know what she was getting into, marrying a politician.

She had discovered that it wasn't so bad after all, not if you could survive those interminable banquets with the dried-out fried chicken. And she felt she was making a difference for a lot of people who were hearing-impaired. Just appearing with David generated interest, and the school had received a lot of good publicity.

Beth nudged her as the vibrations began again in the floor, and they gave each other the thumbs-up sign. Beth began walking slowly down the aisle and Laura waited in the back, looking around the pews lovingly. There was David's family: dear Grendel; Erin — who was bawling already; and Alan's wife, Sonya. Artie was there, too, and Bob Randall. Jean and Mary kept looking excitedly toward the back of the church, and Laura smiled when she saw that Mary's corsage was on sideways.

Anne, Julie, and Karen were on the other side, Clara wide-eyed with anticipation by the aisle. There were other children from the school there as well, signing covertly among themselves. The interpreter who would translate the ceremony into sign language was standing on the left, a nervous smile on her face. And there was Horton sitting in the back pew, looking solemn and dignified.

Laura looked down at the bouquet of pink rosebuds and bridal wreath and took a deep breath. I never thought I could be so happy, she thought. She felt the music swell through the floorboards, and the congregation stood and turned toward her.

She began to walk slowly down the aisle, her eyes fixed on David. He was smiling, and she could see everything in the world she had ever wanted right there in his face.

She crossed the bridge, and she was walking toward David, to join his hearing world with her silent one.

The employees of G.K. Hall hope you have enjoyed this Large Print book. All our Large Print titles are designed for easy reading, and all our books are made to last. Other G.K. Hall books are available at your library, through selected book-stores, or directly from us.

For information about titles, please call:

(800) 223-1244
(800) 223-6121

To share your comments, please write:

Publisher
G.K. Hall & Co.
295 Kennedy Memorial Drive
Waterville, ME 04901